Torn Apart

Jean Klier

ISBN: 0995367604
ISBN-13: 978-0995367609

DEDICATION

Josef and Elisabeth
who loved and nurtured Dieter in his early years

TORN APART is a novel based on a true story

CHAPTER ONE

A lone figure hunched forward against the cold wind. More snow was beginning to fall as he crunched along the footpath with his hands deep in the pockets of his dark greatcoat. On his head he wore a peaked cap with ear muffs tied firmly in place. The collar of his coat was turned up to keep out as much cold as possible. Street lights did their best to dissipate the darkness of the dismal early evening scene but flurries of snow diffused it. At the corner of Grillparzer Street he stopped at an imposing house and pulled the bell cord. Its ring echoed within. His gaze went upwards momentarily to the second storey window. It was a solid stone house, three storeys in all but his heart was held captive by the one in that lighted room. He stamped his feet to get rid of the snow from his boots and warm his toes.

At last the heavy wooden door swung back and there was young Rudi ushering him into the entrance hall. Rudi took his coat and hung it on a hook. He liked Max but usually his big sister Erika took over and he was pushed aside. Rudi led Max through to the living room and announced his arrival to the men. "It's Max back again!"

"Hallo Max. Something to drink?" offered Herr Doerre.

"Yes please. Brrrr it's cold out there. It's beginning to snow again."

"I thought it would. It's been trying hard all day," the man of the house continued.

Max accepted a glass of schnapps and settled down into an armchair. The two older men were smoking pipes, sitting comfortably in their chairs their legs extended toward the stove that warmed the room, while the women's business was being attended to upstairs.

There were three generations of males in the family present in the room, Herr Doerre, his son in law Josef Klier and his two sons, Heinz and Rudi.

"Let's hope the winter snows put a stop to Hitler's lunacy for a while," Josef suggested.

There was silence in the room, dark memories lurking in the corners. "Yes! It makes it difficult living here in Czechoslovakia when he's out for revenge. He doesn't care how it affects us," Heinz said. He had befriended Max at the Bruex Barracks where he was waiting to see what their next move would be, where they would be sent with the German war machine. Heinz had not seen active service yet and had brought Max home to have a meal with his family a while ago. Now upstairs, his sister Erika was giving birth to Max's child. Heinz wondered how that would all work out but it was not his problem. Erika could sort out her own life. She certainly liked the men.

"He should never have killed all the men in Lidice," Max added to the conversation. "He vowed to wade through blood to get Heydrich's killers, but who's to say they were from Lidice," he went on.

"That's right. Now we have to live with the consequences. People look at us with suspicion just because we speak German."

"There's talk out there that Benes wants to return home from London. If he comes to power again we're in trouble. He's trying to get the support of the Red Army. Allow them to occupy our country," said Herr Doerre, a tall well-built man. As Superintendent of Police for the Bruex District he was privy to important information which was crucial to the family if they needed to flee.

"I guess the aim is to get rid of Hitler at any cost!" Heinz joined in.

"I won't be standing around to see how that goes, Son!" warned Josef.

"But where do we go?"

"Over the mountains! Let's hope we've got time. We need to watch and listen carefully," Opa Doerre said.

Frau Hunger finished cleaning up after dinner. She dried her hands on her apron then stoked and damped down the stove for the night. Next she clumped upstairs with another bucket of hot water. She was looking forward to going to her room and putting her feet up. Erika was in labour and she had lost count of the number of times she had been up and down the stairs today. The men were busy downstairs, doing what men do best at such times. Opa Doerre was smoking his pipe, sometimes jabbing the stem of it into the conversation to emphasise a point. Herr Klier was there too and young Max, the father to be. It would be more trouble than it was worth to have him in the birthing room. Although he had been a soldier in Stalingrad, they said, men had weak stomachs when it came to this.

She went quietly into the room and refilled the basin. Frau Klier, Elisabeth, was tending to her daughter, mopping her forehead and rubbing her back. Erika uttered a shrill cry as another pain took hold of her. Heaven sakes, it should not be long now, poor thing. Oma Doerre, Erika's grandmother, was a midwife so she was in good hands. Oma stroked her hand as she spoke soothing words, encouraging her to breathe deeply in between the pains. With her years of experience she felt that the baby would arrive soon. She had worked for Dr Koenig until he and his family disappeared one dark night. The SS had come to the Doerre house looking for him but thank goodness Erika had answered the door and said something to get rid of them or they could all have been in trouble. She wondered what Erika had said so that their family was not implicated in these racially prejudiced times. In the corner of the room with a rug over her knees sat old Oma Matz, nodding with approval at the goings on around her. She was the matriarch of the family. The baby would be the fifth generation to be living under this roof. She hoped Max would marry Erika but time would tell. He certainly seemed to be attentive to her earlier in the evening and could not stand to hear her cries.

Downstairs the air was somewhat foggy from the pipe smoke. The men were enjoying the warmth coming from the furnace in the basement. Heavy curtains shut out the freezing night air. A glass of schnapps warmed them from the inside. At any other time it would have been relaxing but not for Max tonight. He tensed as they heard a loud cry of pain from the room upstairs. How long would his sweetheart have to endure this? He felt helpless and prayed that all would go well and soon. With a pang of guilt his thoughts flicked back to his wife and little daughter at home. He had some decisions to make. In the meantime he would have to tread carefully. Another cry and the murmur of voices, footsteps moving back and forth across the floor. He waited and listened almost holding his breath. At last Frau Klier appeared in the doorway as Max opened it.

"It's a boy, a fine healthy boy!"

"And Erika?"

"She's all right too. You can see her now."

Max rushed up the stairs two at a time and into the room. Erika lay back on the pillows with her dank hair framing her face. She looked exhausted but, my God, she was beautiful cradling their son in her arms. He sank to his knees beside the bed, took her face in his hands and gently kissed her. "It's a boy," she said, holding the tiny wrapped bundle out to Max.

CHAPTER TWO

Erika left Bruex in early 1943 when Dieter was only two months old, leaving him in the care of her parents. Who knows what happened to her lover Max? He had been there for Christmas and for the birth of his son and left about a week later. They did not marry and Erika never talked about him. He was not her first lover and she hoped he would not be the last. She would just need to be more careful next time as she was not ready for the responsibility of looking after a child. She wanted to live the high life in spite of the war.

Dieter, now almost two years old, was happy living with Oma and Opa and the other family members while his mother was away on war duty in Dresden.

"Come on, we've got a job to do." Opa Doerre took his hat from the hook by the back door and put it on. Dieter sidled off the bench and rubbed his hands together to wipe off the crumbs. He loved watching Opa Doerre feed the geese. Just as well he had finished his breakfast in time. Out in the courtyard it was a crisp spring morning. The sun shone down and birds flew overhead. Opa looked up, stretched, took three deep breaths of the morning air. He always did that and Dieter copied. Then they went over to the stable where he kept geese and rabbits.

"Now you hold the spoon while I get the food out." He took oats and semolina from the bins and mixed them together in an old pot. Then he poured in hot water and held out his hand for the spoon. Slowly, carefully he mixed the thick porridge until it was all moist and sticking together. He pulled up his sleeves and sank his hands into the mixture for the final stir. Taking small lumps he rolled them into finger size rolls working quickly and deftly. He had done this for years and knew what he was about.

While Dieter waited he looked at the geese in their cages and made little honking noises as he pretended to flap his wings. Opa

Doerre looked over and smiled. His great grandson might be able to take over this job one day, if they were able to stay here. When everything was ready Opa set the pot down on the cobblestones next to the box that he sat on. He opened the latch and lifted the door on the top of the first cage. As he took out a goose he felt its weight.

"Yes not bad." He sat on the box with the goose held firmly between his knees. It stretched its neck towards the pot of food but Opa was faster. He held its head and opened the beak. Down went the first finger of porridge and another and another. At last he could feel that the crop was full so he put the bird back in the cage. The goose wiggled and made disgruntled noises as it preened its ruffled feathers. Opa fed each of the geese in turn. Then he stood back and admired his handiwork.

He took Dieter by the hand to lead him inside.

"We'll have a fat goose for Christmas."

Opa Doerre also had a garden. It was way up on the legendary Schlossberg, next to the castle. In fact it butted up to the castle. On the other three sides the garden was contained by a latticed paling fence. There he grew an abundance of peas and beans in the summer. A hut stood in the corner. When there was a heap of work to be done in the garden Opa Doerre slept the night there, ready to start bright and early the next morning. He enjoyed the peace and quiet of such times. He sat on a box leaning back against the summer house, breathing in the mountain air and soaking up the first rays of the sun as the mist left the valleys. He had a bread board on his knee with a bread roll, sausage and a thick slice of cheese. Beside him on the ground sat a mug of buttermilk. As he surveyed the garden he ate a leisurely breakfast. Two blackbirds eyed him from the top of the fence before hopping down to look for grubs and worms for their own morning meal. They scritched and scratched among the mulch to find their repast. Oh, well, time to begin work before the heat of the day. Firstly he went to the well to get water for the seedlings that were just coming through the ground over by the hut. He would need to plant them out in a couple of weeks the way the weather was becoming warmer. Tomatoes, cabbage, lettuce, cauliflower and broccoli. Next he attended to the peas and beans to make sure they were hanging on tight as they climbed the lattice. He heaped the soil around the mounds where the potatoes grew. It should be a good crop this year. The rows of carrots, parsnips and beetroot needed to be thinned and he laid the carrots that were big enough for the kitchen under the shade of the white and red currant bushes. He cut a cabbage and some kohlrabi from his winter garden and put it all together. His daughter Elisabeth would come and bring his midday meal. Usually she brought her little grandson Dieter with her too. Opa Doerre went back to cleaning the beds of the winter crop, digging in compost as he went. This was where he planned to plant the seedlings.

Elisabeth wound her way up the path holding Dieter's hand. He was a sturdy little boy. If Rudi had been with her Dieter could have had a piggy back.

"Oma, ride please," he appealed with his big blue eyes.

"Not today, Dieterle. I have to carry Opa's dinner. Let's have a rest." She led him over to a wayside seat made from a log and they sat down. Placing the basket beside her she drew Dieter's attention to the birds overhead and the rapid rat-a-tat-tat of a distant woodpecker. Then they headed up to the garden once more. Opa Doerre looked up as the garden gate announced their arrival with a squeak. The time had flown but he was certainly ready for a meal. He washed his hands in a bucket of water and splashed some onto his face as well.

"What's for dinner today? I'm ravenous." Elisabeth removed the well-wrapped dish from her basket and put it on the table. She could feel the warmth from it as she took off the lid. Then she ladled the stew into bowls and cut thick slices of freshly baked bread.

"Mmm, smells good," he said appreciatively, as they began to eat. Once they had finished Elisabeth poured warm coffee from a flask and handed a mug to her father. Then she passed Dieter a cup of raspberry juice and they took their drinks outside to sit on the bench and look at her father's handiwork. Dieter was soon finished and jumped down. He found a stick and trailed it behind him as he ran up and down the garden paths. Elisabeth and her father talked about the garden and admired the flowers he had planted amongst the vegetables.

"I've put some vegetables under the bush for you to take home. Pick some flowers too if you like." He filled his pipe and sat back contentedly to survey the scene. An eagle soared overhead, wheeling this way and that as it spread powerful wings on the air currents. In the distance a cuckoo called and another echoed a reply. A shiver went down his spine as the thought came to him. Why was the mighty eagle behaving like a cuckoo and invading others' nests?

CHAPTER THREE

Elisabeth was beside herself with worry. Before Christmas 1944 her brother Herbert had gone missing. Josef had gone to his men's hairdressing salon to seek information regarding his whereabouts. The shop was closed and his neighbour said two Nazi soldiers in uniform had called on Herbert and he was taken away. He had not been seen or heard of since. Josef knew it was useless to go and ask questions as it would only incriminate the rest of the family. He went home with a heavy heart. Elisabeth sobbed and shuddered as Josef enfolded her in his strong arms and told her what he had learned. About a month later a sealed coffin with a small viewing slide had been delivered to Grillparzer Street. It contained Herbert's body for them to identify with strict instructions not to open the coffin. How long had he been incarcerated and tortured? What was his crime? Having a Jewish heritage? That was the only possible answer as he was a fine upstanding citizen.

Afterwards the family lived in fear and trembling. They were part of a strong Jewish community that had coexisted in Bohemia in harmony with the Czech population for generations. The trouble started after Hitler's henchmen wiped out the village of Lidice in retribution for the murder of one of his generals in early June 1942. Many Sudetenlanders felt it was important to keep on side and joined the Nazi Party, creating the strongest following throughout the German Empire, but not the family in Grillparzer Street. Later that year Dr Koenig and his family had vanished overnight. Then their friend Herr Soukob who was a furniture maker and owned a factory in Bruex had met the same fate in 1944 along with his wife and children. The only safeguard for the Doerre / Klier household was the fact that both Opa Doerre and Josef Klier held responsible positions in the community. Opa Doerre was the Commissioner of Police and passersby always doffed their caps to him. His son in law,

Josef was Inspector of Mines. The safety of the coalminers in the whole province depended on his attention to detail. As they went about their duties they took time to listen to the men, keeping a finger on the pulse of the political beast. They had decided that the Klier family would flee if necessary, leaving the older members behind. They would not be seen as a threat and crossing the mountain pass would be too arduous for them. They tried to keep their heads down and go about their daily routines efficiently and quietly. It was impossible to guess where the Nazi Party would strike next. In early 1945 Josef's sister Mitzi went missing. They could only pray that she had not met a similar fate.

CHAPTER FOUR

Erika enjoyed life in Dresden. In the city she lived upstairs in an apartment which she shared with two other young women from work. Each day she walked to the telephone exchange where she was helping the Nazi war machine with communications to the south of the Eastern Front. Here she was free of the responsibilities of mothering her child – at nineteen she had not been ready for that. Life in Dresden offered more opportunities for a social life in spite of the shortages caused by war. Her job was secure – she was needed.

Lately she had heard talk that all was not well in Sudetenland where her family and little son lived. Sometimes she missed them and felt a pang of guilt if she thought of Dieter. Then too she heard disturbing news that things were not good with the German forces. Hungary had declared war on Germany and the Soviet Union had pushed into the occupied territories of Poland and Silesia. Perhaps she should ask for leave to go and see her family. Or maybe it would be wiser just to go and let her friends cover for her. Then she could look up Max. Erika began to make her plans. She stuffed her meager belongings into a bag and dressed in her comfortable clothes for travel. She took her long dark woollen coat from the wardrobe and put it on. A quick look in the mirror to check her wavy hair before tying it down with a scarf. Now a note for her flat mates: 'Sorry to leave like this. Urgent matters to attend to at home. See you in two weeks. Erika.' She left it on the kitchen table under a mug. Erika pulled on woollen gloves as she opened the door, picked up her bag and ran down the stairs onto the street.

The city was going about its daily business oblivious to the young woman striding out towards the railway station. She knew a train was scheduled in half an hour but even German punctuality was questionable in time of war. At three in the afternoon she guessed that there would not be too many travellers, probably a few soldiers.

Her breath formed a cloud in the cold air. As she rounded the corner into Bahnhof Street there was the station. Thank goodness, her bag was getting awfully heavy. People were milling around. Two soldiers lounging by the steps, smoking, eyed Erika up and down as she went into the station. One made a comment and the other laughed as she walked on pretending to take no notice. She went to the ticket counter, checked the time for the next train to Sudetenland, took her leather purse from her pocket and paid for it. So far so good! With fifteen minutes to wait she leaned against the wall of the platform, her bag at her feet. She hoped that there would be no delays – you never could tell. Her mind drifted back to Dieter. He was two years old now. Who would he look like? Herself or Max? She had had little contact with her family for so long – needed to get on and live the life of a young woman. That was reasonable surely! She wondered what her mother would say about her attitude. Well, too bad, she didn't intend to change it now. She did not plan on getting pregnant again and anyway Max was as much to blame as her.

At last she heard the whistle of the train as it thundered into the station in a cloud of fury. She was surprised by the crowd of people and troops already on board. She elbowed her way past a group of soldiers and clambered on amid their ribald comments. In the corner of the carriage was an empty seat. She sank onto it and rested back on the slats, her bag clasped on her knee. Out the window last minute to-ing and fro-ing. Fond farewells of a mother and son in uniform. The guard blew his whistle for everyone to stand back as he slammed the door. The train hissed and booped in reply then lurched forward.

"Do you mind if I sit here?" Erika was broken from her reverie by one of the soldiers she had seen near the station.

"Suit yourself." At least he was the better looking one of the two.

"Going far?" he asked.

"I'm off to Bruex. Going home for a bit. What about you?"

"I've had enough of war. I'm going home too."

She settled further into the seat and watched the landscape slide by. The train clackety-clacked on and they were lulled into silence.

"War is a waste" the soldier announced out of the blue.

"I agree," said Erika.

"What's your name?"

"Erika, and yours?"

"Werner."

They chatted on for a bit. Werner had been fighting in Odessa and "taken leave" he said. Whatever that meant. It did not pay to ask questions in war. The train hurtled on, rattling its way to Chemnitz. Night began to descend around them. The winter sky darkened. Erika drew her coat round her legs and shivered.

"You cold?" he asked.

"A bit."

"I can keep you warm."

"Yeah?" He put his arm around her. Erika did not protest.

"Want a smoke?" he asked.

"No thanks."

"Mind if I do?" She shook her head. He lit a cigarette and puffed the smoke into the air. The train changed rhythm. Another station? No, it seemed to be stopping in the middle of nowhere. The wheels squealed and the engine hissed as they ground to a halt.

"What now?"

"Who knows?" The guard walked through to announce "a stop for some time." Whatever that meant. Why couldn't he be more precise?

"Let's stretch our legs," said Werner. They climbed down onto the rough ground beside the tracks, Werner helping her from the last step. He tucked her hand under his arm and she found the warmth comforting. The cold night air was interrupted by a snort from the engine and a puff of smoke. Groups of passengers dotted the tracks, talking, asking questions for which there were no answers. Erika and Werner wandered up and down. Thank goodness for the moon.

Suddenly the sky was disturbed by planes high overhead. They droned lazily on. "Wonder what they're up to. Some poor bastards," Werner said.

"Yes!" Erika shivered. He put his arm round her and drew her closer. They stood in silence looking into the indigo sky. No one had anything to say. A violent flash lit the sky. Seconds later a boom hit their ears. Shock, horror! It continued on till the sky was blood red. Everyone began talking at once. Erika sagging at the knees, sank into Werner's arms. Dresden had been hit. It was alight. She was on the last train out. Thank God! But what of her flat mates?

There was more disturbing news for Erika when she reached Bruex. Max had gone off with his regiment after months at the Barracks, twiddling their thumbs or doing what soldiers do when they are not at the front. Heinz could not say where he had gone, even if he knew. Not one to sit around and wait, Erika took matters into her own hands and went to the Standesamt to change Dieter's family name on his birth certificate from Klier (her maiden name) to Koch (Werner's surname). It could be useful later if Max never came back or returned to his wife and daughter. She was shrewd to the point of deviousness and made sure that no one else knew about it, not even Werner! Before long Erika became bored with the restrictions of life in Bruex and family expectations that she would care for her son while she was home. After a battle of wills she stated her intentions loudly and clearly and left without a tear in her eye or a promise to return soon.

CHAPTER FIVE

"Just in time! We were about to set off without you." Oma had changed Dieter and he was clean and tidy with his hair slicked back. Heinz and Rudi were waiting. Quickly Opa changed out of his work boots, combed his hair and put on his good coat and hat. It was late afternoon in March 1945 and the evening chill was moving in as they left the house and headed for Wenzelskirche. Men were trudging home from work in the mines but otherwise the streets were empty. Opa carried Dieter in his arms. It was faster that way. As they rounded the corner there stood the church. It was a grey stone edifice built in late Gothic style. Tall windows along the side were like sentinels who had kept watch for almost four hundred years. Small openings studded the roof allowing in more light. It was a solid yet majestic structure, its spire catching the last rays of the setting sun.

Heinz opened the heavy wooden door, putting his boot against it, while the men removed their hats and the family filed in. Sunlight fizzled through the leadlight windows but did nothing to warm the place before it sank below the hill. A musty smell of incense pervaded the air. The priest came forward from the altar to greet them and lead them to the baptismal font at the rear of the church. Dieter's gaze wandered from the vaulted arches and the paintings of saints around the gallery, back to the priest and family as they began to talk in low reverent tones. He had not been here before. He did not know why they were here now but he felt secure in Opa's arms as the priest began to intone the rite of baptism. Oma was relieved when it had been arranged. Everyone needed to have their documents in order these days. It was important that Dieter had his baptismal certificate too. It had not seemed important earlier and she had expected Erika to see to all this when she came home. In the end she realized that they would have to do it themselves. Little did she know what Erika had done in her official capacity as mother on her flying visit to Bruex less than a month ago. They did not know where she was now. What would become of her! She brought her mind back to the present as the priest sprinkled holy water on Dieter's head and made the sign of the cross over him. Dear God keep him safe.

"In the name of the Father and the Son and the Holy Spirit, Amen." Then he took them through to the vestry to complete the baptismal certificate. He signed his name with a flourish and applied the church stamp to it with a finality that announced that everything was now in order. Opa shook his hand and thanked him for helping them. The priest ushered them out into the cold night air. They heard the door shut behind them. As they retraced their steps Dieter snuggled into Opa's coat and felt Opa's strong arms holding him close.

At last they reached home. As they opened the door the welcome smell of cooking wafted from the kitchen and the warmth of the house enveloped them. Opa and Oma went into the sitting room. He slid his hand behind books on the bookcase and retrieved a small key. With it he opened a drawer in the dresser and slipped the certificate in with those of the rest of the family. He closed the drawer, turned the key, returning it to its hiding place.

"Well that's that then,' Opa said.

"Yes, but let's hope we don't need them."

"After both Herbert and Mitzi going missing I think that is a vain hope," he replied softly.

CHAPTER SIX

Rudi knew exactly what to do when the air raid siren sounded. He could hear his mother's voice in his head.

"Put on your warm coat and hat and take the rucksack. You know where it is kept. Then wake Dieter up and wrap him in his woollen rug. Put him in the rucksack and put it on your back. Don't worry if he cries, he'll soon go back to sleep. Next get Oma Matz and make sure she puts her coat on. Take her on your arm and head for the bunker as quickly as possible."

"Yes Mamma."

Rudi was only thirteen but strong. He was pleased when his parents had given him this responsibility but he had no time for such thoughts now. Quickly Rudi donned his thick outer layer and grabbed the rucksack. Dieter was sound asleep in his bed oblivious to the wailing of the sirens. Rudi took Dieter's rug from the end of the bed, murmuring apologies as he wrapped him in it and stuffed Dieter into the rucksack. It was easier to do when he was still half asleep and docile. Then he went through to Oma Matz's bedroom. She too was fast asleep and extremely deaf. Rudi rocked her back and forth and she woke up with a start. It was no use talking to her so he helped her to sit up and lifted the covers for her to swing her legs over the side of the bed.

"What for are you doing this?" Although the family had talked about it many times she still did not remember when woken from her dreams in the middle of the night. Rudi knew it was pointless arguing with his great grandmother.

"Come!" he urged.

He helped her into her long woollen coat and tied her scarf under her chin. Taking her by the arm he led her downstairs. The heavy front door shut with a thump behind them.

"Where are we going?"

"Listen, can you hear that?" Rudi turned and mouthed the words carefully close to her ear.

"I can't hear anything." Rudi pressed her arm firmly against his ribs as they scuttled through the streets in the dark night. A sliver of moon peering from behind a cloud was the only light.

"Along Grillparzer Street and turn left towards the mines. The bunker is at the end of the street," Mamma had instructed.

Of course he knew where it was, he passed it every day on his way to school! Anyway there were crowds of people now, coming out of their houses and scurrying along, keeping close to the buildings as if somehow they could hide from the planes and the bombs. Rudi, Dieter and Oma Matz were swept along with them. In the distance above the roof line they could see flashes of light followed by explosions.

"Boom, boom," echoed Dieter in the rucksack. He did not talk much. There was no need with so many adults in the house but this was as clear as a bell. He wriggled and leaned sideways to see where they were going, almost catching Rudi off balance. Rudi shrugged his shoulders to settle his burden in a more comfortable position as they descended the wide stone steps into the bunker like scared rabbits diving for safety. It was almost as cold as outside. The underground haven was lit by bright lights, a stark contrast to the inky blackness above. Rudi took the first passage on the right and found a bunk to rest his bundle. He helped Dieter to wriggle out of the rucksack and wrapped him in the blanket, making sure there were no toes peeping out. He sat beside him and stroked his head. Gradually his big eyes closed and he was asleep once more. Oma Matz had found a spot for herself too but she was resting, watching everyone else talking in hushed tones that she could not hear. Rudi hoped that she would not go to sleep because then he would have to go through the whole rigmarole again. At least she would not get too comfortable on these bunks. Rudi leant back against the cold stone wall and put his feet up on the bed next to Dieter. It would not be too long before the all clear was given, he hoped. The ground shook with a "BOOM" close by. Was Father safe? He was a warden who shepherded others to safety before he sought refuge himself. Rudi was told not to worry about the rest of the family.

"Just get Oma and Dieter to the bunker. We'll meet back at home afterwards." This had been going on for several months now and so far so good. But that last single boom seemed closer than before. Was it just his imagination? Was the war getting to him? He did not know and he could do nothing about it.

Rudi woke with a start as a warden poked his head round the door and called, "All clear." He must have dozed off. With the flurry of activity Oma Matz roused too and watched while Rudi manoeuvered Dieter's sleeping form into the rucksack. She took his arm as they trudged homewards. The moon sidled out once more to continue on its way across the night sky. As they turned into Grillparzer Street Rudi saw people clustered on the footpath near their house. Father was there safe and well but the house next door had suffered damage from the "boom" that had shaken the ground. It was not a direct hit but the house was now uninhabitable. The roof had caved in and the walls huddled inwards with nothing to support any longer. The real damage had occurred further down the street where only rubble remained.

"They were trying to wipe out the mines!"

"Well they missed. But what is worse, no livelihood or no home?"

Rudi saw Papa pointing to their home. The roof had lifted slightly with the explosion then settled back on top of a cracked wall.

"It'll be fine Rudi. You take Dieter and Oma in to bed. We'll look at it closely tomorrow and see what's to do about it." He patted Rudi's shoulder. "I'll be in soon, son."

CHAPTER SEVEN

It was April 1945. The family prepared for a walk in the forest. Dieter enjoyed these walks. Oma often took him when she collected mushrooms, using her large striped apron, with a knot tied in it for a hold-all. Dieter would help to search them out and Oma plucked them with her big strong hands. He could almost smell them cooking as his taste buds began to tingle. But today was different. Dieter felt the somber mood as they had said their tearful goodbyes to the older generations earlier, not knowing whether they would ever see them again. The whole family was getting ready – Opa, Oma, Rudi, Heinz and Liesl. Oma wrapped Dieter's heavy brown coat around him, buttoning it under his chin. Next she fastened his cloth helmet with the black shiny button. Opa and Heinz donned rucksacks packed with food from the pantry. Cheese, bread and sausage. This was to be no ordinary stroll through the forest. Oma took in the ambience of the kitchen for the last time and with a sigh she walked out holding Dieter firmly by the hand. Opa shut the door.

They walked through the back streets of the city with no comment and headed for the forest up on the hill. As they wound up the track they caught glimpses of the Schloss perched on top like an eagle on its nest. At a fork in the path they veered off to the left, heading towards the north through the forests and fields, small towns and villages towards Berlin. Trees were beginning to sprout buds, adding a touch of normality to their grave situation. Finally they came to the Spree, a river of some size which meandered through the gorge. There was not much water in it now but it would be a torrent after snow melt. Oma put the thought aside. They would probably never see that again. Dieter chattered away with little response from the others. He liked to explore and fossick among the roots of the trees, looking for the little people who lived there. But not today, there was no opportunity for that with Oma holding his hand. As they hurried on his short little legs became tired and he begged for a rest. Rudi bent and scooped him up onto his back as they continued. They headed north up and down the track wending their way through the trees which became thicker now.

Suddenly Opa stopped and frantically gestured to them to scramble down the bank towards the river. Rudi passed Dieter to Heinz and slid hurriedly down to the shelter of the trees among the rocks. Liesel scrabbled behind them. Oma shoved her hand over Dieter's mouth and put a warning finger to her lips to silence him as she pushed him against the bank. All was quiet then he heard the sound of heavy feet on the path above. Opa pointed up and Dieter's wide eyes followed his finger. A line of dull black mud encrusted boots marched past, scrunching on the detritus along the track. Dieter questioned Oma with his eyes but she did not respond only prayed to God that he would remain quiet till the threat had passed. It seemed like forever before the boots retreated in the distance. Only then could they relax a little and continue on their way towards - who knew where? Away from the town where they were in danger and away from the soldiers just following orders.

So it began. They were homeless now. It would not be safe to go back. The alienation that Hitler started was completed with the invasion of the Red Army. This was what they feared would happen, what they had planned for, in case it happened. They had stayed till the last moment, hoping against hope that they would not have to flee their homeland where five generations lived. Opa carried the small wooden box in his rucksack where he had meticulously gathered all their personal documents over the past year – birth certificates, baptismal certificates and their marriage certificate. Elisabeth had insisted that he include family photos too.

"The documents will travel better if the box is full!"

"I will travel better if my pack is not too full." Finally Elisabeth had won out. Josef could not resist her pleading.

They pushed on. Opa prayed that was the last of the soldiers.

"Mind you," he said, "They won't meet with any resistance. That's probably all the manpower they need."

"They've been invited after all." Oma sighed. They trudged on in silence, each one deep in thought.

"Are we there yet?" a small voice piped up.

"Not yet, Dieterle."

"Where are we going?"

"Away from the soldiers! We'll find somewhere to sleep before it gets dark," Oma comforted.

"Are the bombs coming?"

"No Dieterle, the bombs are finished." That was the only reason Dieter knew for being out after dark. It was difficult for a little fellow to understand what was happening. He was not three years old yet. They wound their way up the pass through the Erzgebirge, known as the Ore Mountains, rich in minerals. Opa knew that if they followed the Spree River it would lead them through to Germany. Only seventy kilometers as the eagle flies but trudging round up and over the mountains would make it considerably longer. Leaves fluttered down around them as a breeze ruffled through the trees. It was picturesque at this time of year with the sun filtering through near naked branches. The smell of damp foliage underfoot wafted up but the family walked on, not seeming to notice.

Opa was thankful they had escaped before the snow melt started. He had waited as long as possible but was aware that it would be more difficult to cross streams and mountains into Germany if they left it too late. It was difficult enough of a challenge with a young child but mud and slush would have made it even more arduous. He looked around as they walked. Birds twittered excitedly - about what? Were they communicating what they had seen and done that day? Had they seen the soldiers? But then they were just more people to the birds he supposed. At least they had somewhere to roost, a place where they felt comfortable and at home. He scanned the valleys that forked off to the right and left of them. There were no signs of habitation anywhere. He had hoped they could shelter in a barn. The Erzgebirge were not high mountains and surely there should be a farm nearby with cows or goats that could feed on wildflowers in the meadows. But he had to take a chance on that. The family had gone about their business as usual, trying not to arouse suspicion. They had been self-sufficient as far as fruit and vegetables were concerned, eggs and some meat too. Josef thought of his father-in-law feeding the geese and rabbits that in turn fed them! What about his parents? Would they ever see them again? The future was uncertain and their parents were ageing.

At last Opa saw what he was looking for, a barn perched low on the side of a hill. He crouched down and pointed it out to Dieter.

"That's where we're sleeping tonight. In amongst the warm dry straw. I'm sure the animals won't mind."

Dieter looked. He was hungry and tired and now they could rest. He could not understand what was going on but he felt the sadness of the rest of the family. Opa picked him up as they left the path and headed towards the shelter. There was no farm house here – it must be in the next valley, thank goodness. This way they did not have to explain. You did not know who you could trust these days.

Heinz lifted the wooden latch and pulled the door. It creaked open and the breeze stirred the hay scattered over the floor. The smell of hay reminded him of Opa Doerre and the animals he kept. Dieter peered into the gloom, his eyes adjusting to the dimness inside, even darker than the fading light outside. A bird rose from the rafters and squawked away.

"It's all right. They just didn't expect any visitors at this time of day." Opa walked in and looked around. The loft would be the place to sleep. Clean dry straw and up there it should be warmer.

" Rudi, would you refill the water flasks."

"Yes Mamma." He picked up the flasks and headed out the door.

"Don't be long, it'll soon be dark."

He was a good boy. Only fourteen but responsible. You could rely on Rudi to get a job done. Oma set about preparing beds in the straw while a little light remained. Heinz helped Dieter up the ladder to have a look.

"Where am I sleeping?" Dieter asked.

"Right here next to me."

"I like that nest." Dieter lay down in the hay to try it out.

"Yes little sparrow, you'll sleep well. But let's have some food first," Oma said.

She heard the door open. Rudi was back. Soon his head appeared at the top of the ladder with a grin on his face.

"Would you like eggs for breakfast?"

"Where did you get eggs?"

"The farmhouse is in a little nook in the next valley. I went looking for running water and there it was. So I went to investigate. It wasn't my fault that they didn't collect the eggs today."

"You're lucky you didn't get caught. What did the hens have to say about it?" asked Heinz.

"Very little. I was quieter than a fox and not so smelly."

"You need to be careful," his mother replied. She smiled to herself. Rudi would be an asset if he continued like this but she did not want him in danger.

"How will we cook them?" Rudi asked.

"We won't!" said his father. "Can't run the risk and we have no pots and pans."

"We can soak our bread in them. Look," Oma cracked the top off an egg carefully and dipped a finger of bread into it. She handed it to Dieter. "Eat Dieterle." He needed no second prompting. The others followed his example, eating sausage, egg and bread. The cheese would keep for another time with the rest of the bread. It would travel better than fresh eggs. And so, replete after their meal and a drink of water, the family nestled into the straw. The straw tickled Dieter's cheek a little but he did not mind. He pretended he was baby Jesus in the manger, just like the painting in the church with all the people looking on. He snuggled down with Oma's arm over him, soon drifting off to sleep with the murmur of human voices around him. Oma and Opa were talking about their journey.

"I was wondering whether we'd have to sleep under the stars," Opa said.

"We are fortunate. Many people don't have even this."

CHAPTER EIGHT

They had covered many kilometers by now, not knowing where the next meal would come from or when. Where would they sleep? Dieter walked from time to time but his short legs soon became tired. Then one of the men carried him, if you could call Heinz and Rudi men too. But then that is what war did to people. Young boys and girls who should have been still at school had responsibilities thrust upon them. Dieter liked to sit on Rudi's shoulders best of all. Then he had a good view of the world around him. Rudi talked to him and sometimes they laughed. Liesel was too young to carry Dieter and Oma held his hand when he walked. That way he did not wander off dreaming.

They had crossed the Erzgebirge and wound down to civilization of sorts in Germany! They followed the lie of the land towards the towns and cities. As they went they saw the impact of war on the lives of innocent people. Hordes that were homeless and hungry like them, some sick or injured, old and young alike. Mostly they headed for a city hoping for a train so that they could take a rest from endless walking. They trudged in silence each group fending for themselves. So the Klier family arrived in Chemnitz.

Opa surveyed the city. All around was evidence of bombings earlier in the year. Not the devastation that they would see later but still much worse than they had left behind in Bruex. On the horizon he could see parts of factories in the industrial area sticking up at all angles like decaying teeth in unhealthy gums. But he was not here to inspect the damage. They were here to see if trains were running to move them on to find a new home. It was late morning and the sky was overcast. A cold wind blew from the north. A man lounged against a building. Opa asked for directions to the station.

"There!" he pointed round the corner.

It was dim in the station with no lights. Dispirited people were talking in monotones, babies crying and a man stomped up and down trying to warm his feet. The smell hit them as they walked in. The body odour from a large group of unwashed people herded into a small area. They were like a mob of sheep huddled in a pen keeping a wary eye out for the sheep dog. Oma found a sheltered corner on the platform and sank down to rest with Dieter snuggled up beside her. Opa went to see what information he could decipher from the rumours flying around, maybe from a station master. If a train came it would be a scramble, he knew. He scanned the crowd looking for someone in authority when he heard, "Papa!" He turned around slowly. Heaven knew there were many papas here. He was stunned as Erika threw herself at him. Where had she come from? Fancy meeting her like this, here. She had Werner in tow grinning sheepishly as Opa questioned his daughter. He worried about her but she did not seem to worry about them too much.

"Your son is just over there."

He led them over to his wife. Tears of relief flowed as mother and daughter hugged each other. "Where have you been?" her mother asked. "We were worried about you."

"Here and there like everyone else."

"Thank God you're alive."

Erika smiled and patted her son's head.

"How's little Dieter?"

Dieter peered from behind Oma's skirts.

"A kiss for Mutti?"

Dieter stood on tip toes to kiss the cheek turned towards him.

"That's my boy! My word you're getting big."

Dieter retreated again and watched from a safe distance. Mother and daughter talked on about where they had been and what they had been doing. Dieter watched a family of children squabbling over a piece of bread. Their mother cuffed one around the ears and that set up a loud wailing. Suddenly Opa came back insisting that they move forward.

"A train! Quick!" They scrambled to their feet and surged forward with everyone else. Erika grabbed Dieter's hand and hoisted him into her arms. Then she pushed her way along the platform to the front of the train. Werner followed in her wake. Unfortunately what she had not bargained for were the passengers already on the train before it pulled in. There was definitely no space at all in the front carriages. She turned to Werner in despair.

"What to do now?"

"Come with me."

They went round the front of the train and Werner pointed to a wide ledge below the boiler. He helped Erika to step across from the platform and handed Dieter up to her.

"The best view of all," he said as he jumped up beside them.

"Is it safe?"

"Of course. Keep your feet up and hang on to Dieter."

Dieter looked around in awe. He had never seen a train this close before. It towered behind them, breathing out steam, hissing and snorting. He snuggled against his mother for reassurance. Soon the engine began to make more noise as the station master blew his whistle. Slowly the monster moved forward, getting up steam to take this mass of humanity to their next destination. Wherever that might be! It depended whether the tracks were twisted and distorted from the air raids. Out past the bombed buildings they went and into the countryside. Dieter turned his head sideways to see as they gathered speed. It was cold and he began to whimper. Erika turned the sleeves down over his hands and wrapped her coat around him. The roar of the engine and the clackety – clack of the wheels on the tracks drowned out all other sounds. Gradually Dieter was lulled into sleep, dreaming of dragons breathing fire and threatening to swallow up little people. Erika patted him under her coat when he became restless and looked at Werner. Conversation was virtually impossible as they moved along thankful for the best view on the train but not knowing what they would do when nightfall came. Occasionally Erika peered inside her coat at Dieter sleeping. He must have been very tired, poor little mite.

At last he woke. Where was he? What was that noise? Where was Oma? He struggled to sit up and began to cry loudly. Erika put her cold hand on his forehead and he wailed louder.

"He's very hot."

Werner cupped his hand to his ear. She mouthed the words slowly and shouted louder.

"He needs water."

Werner shrugged his shoulders and looked around.

"So?"

"He needs water. You'll have to get some," she screamed above the engine.

"There's none here."

"Well find some!"

Werner sat stubbornly, with shoulders hunched and arms folded tightly across his chest. She must be mad! Why didn't she leave Dieter with her mother? He was not his child.

"He needs water."

"Well you get some!" He held out his hands to take the child and Erika started to pass him over. She had a determined look in her eye and Werner knew what that meant. Dieter cried louder and Mutti relented. Thank God! He would rather get the dratted water than hold a squirming yelling child.

He stood to his feet hanging onto the fastenings on the front of the boiler. He peered to the left of the engine, sidled along to the other side and inspected that too. He could see steam coming from an outlet. Opening his eyes wide in mock terror and with a grimace on his face he disappeared from view.

It was no picnic crawling along a narrow ledge towards the outlet. The shelf was for use when the engine was stationary and so there were few handholds. It was meant for the maintenance engineer to stand on. Werner hoped Erika was worried about him. She had been quite happy to leave Dieter with her parents before so why the sudden interest now? There were some things about her he did not understand. The train suddenly lurched around a curve and Werner swore as he clutched tightly to the ledge. Keep your mind on the job, man, he cautioned himself. Sliding one knee along in front of the other then bringing the other knee up to the boot in front he finally made it. He took a water flask from his jacket pocket. Holding the flask in one hand he gripped the top in his teeth and pulled out the stopper. He found a bolt to hang onto as he leaned down and held the flask over the steam outlet. He prayed for no more lurches as he waited for a decent amount of water to fill the flask. In spite of his bravado in front of Erika he definitely did not intend to repeat the stunt. He nearly fell off in fright as the train whistle sounded. BOOOOOP! He looked up at the cab and there was the driver grinning at him. He tapped his head to show that he thought Werner was crazy. Yes, he might be right but there was no need to scare the daylights out of him. Bastard! At last he decided enough was enough.

He pushed the stopper back into the flask, returned it to his pocket and pressed it down some more. He didn't want to waste a drop. Slowly he sidled backwards the way he had come, reversing around to the front ledge.

Erika gave a sigh of relief as she reached for the flask he offered.

"Where did you get it?"

"Round there."

"You were ages," she shouted.

"I talked to the driver."

She shook her head as Dieter drank thirstily.

Later that afternoon the train slowed. It pulled into a station to stock up on coal and water and see if any more people could cram into the train. Werner and Erika grabbed the chance to fight their way inside the train. People got up to go to the toilet so Erika managed to find a seat with Dieter on her knee. There was standing room only for Werner but it was good to stretch his legs after being cramped on the ledge for so long. At least they were inside for the night ride.

CHAPTER NINE

Two days later the train slowed to a halt. There was no station in sight and speculation was high. No one was keen to run the risk of losing their precious seat so everyone voiced their thoughts.

"Maybe we've run out of steam."

"Not likely. There could be a train coming the other way."

A roar of laughter followed. Finally Werner decided to find out. He jumped to the ground and walked to the front of the train. The engineer was walking back along the track towards him.

"What's the trouble?"

"The line is out not far from here." He pointed to the tracks as he continued, "and it's twisted here. Not safe to continue. You'll have to walk."

"How far to the next station?"

"Salzgitter? About ten kilometers."

There was nothing for it. Werner returned to the carriage and told Erika the news. The sooner they set off the sooner they would get to Salzgitter. With resignation born from their desperate plight people shouldered their few belongings and set off in groups beside the tracks. It was fun for Dieter at first out in the fresh air running along beside Mutti but he soon tired. Mutti carried him for a while until she felt exhausted from little sleep and not enough food. She put him down and he whined and whimpered. Impatiently Werner picked him up. Why couldn't she have left him with his grandparents? He set off with Erika but gradually lagged behind. After some time Erika turned around. She could not see Werner anywhere. What was he playing at? Her gaze glanced along the stream of people behind her, each one doggedly following the one in front. He was not there. She looked ahead. She had not noticed him pass her but maybe he had while she had been plodding, just putting one foot in front of the other. There was no sign of him anywhere. Now she was worried. He seemed to resent Dieter and was impatient with him. She looked out over the ploughed paddocks to the right and left of the tracks. There he was striding back towards her. He must have needed a pee! But hang on a minute, where was Dieter? Behind Werner a little bundle was dumped on the ground.

She ran towards Werner screaming, "My son! Where's my son?"

"I'm sick of him. You look after him if you must!"

Dieter came running towards her holding up his arms. She gathered him up and cradled him protectively.

"How could you do that to my child?"

"You didn't care about him before! Why the sudden interest now?"

Werner turned around and marched back to the line of nomads. Erika tried to keep pace over the furrows, remonstrating with him like a terrier yapping at his heels.

"You needn't think I'm taking responsibility for another man's brat." Finally they walked together in silence, scanning the long line for Oma and Opa to take over once again. From then on Dieter traveled with Oma and Opa and his uncles and aunt. His mother had decided that Werner was more important just now. Dieter would be better off with her parents so Erika and Werner took off in a different direction.

CHAPTER TEN

At last the family group made it to Hannover. Long trestles had been set up along the station platform and people with red crosses on their arm bands were serving mugs of steaming black tea. Opa went in front and the rest of the family followed until they had inched their way forward to the table. As the Red Cross workers poured their tea Oma asked where she could get food for Dieter. It was bad enough for the adults to go hungry but for a growing child who could not understand what was going on, it was worse. He did not have much stamina anymore and had to be carried more often. It broke her heart to see him like that.

"I'm sorry we have nothing. There are too many people and we don't have the resources." She shook her head and turned to serve the next person. Opa took Oma's arm and led her away.

"There's a camp for displaced persons in the street behind the school I've been told. It's very crowded but at least we will have somewhere to sleep while we scout around for food."

She nodded through tear-filled eyes, afraid that her voice would give her away if she spoke. She must be brave and struggle on. They were all in this together through no fault of their own. The hordes of people had dispersed somewhat now as they moved out into the sunlit streets. The warmth felt good on their backs but it highlighted the devastation and despair left behind by the punishing planes of vengeance. Stark shadows lurked behind the twisted remains. People milled about with no purpose, looking at the passersby from sunken eyes. Buildings attempted to stand in the middle of the chaos. The family plodded on and eventually found the camp. Army barracks squatted on a large field. A long queue wound its way towards the gate. Babies cried, hungry children whined, mothers scolded but many stared vacantly ahead, too exhausted to bother, shuffling along as the queue moved forward.

Once inside the family trudged through the camp looking for room in the huts. They were so crowded already. Opa suggested they head for the last row of huts and see what was there.

"Well goodness me! There's a line of latrines here."

Sure enough there was room for them to squeeze into a hut with an elderly couple who had just taken up residence amongst the throng. Raised wooden platforms provided a place to sleep, about two hundred per hut. A cast iron stove stood at the far end, waiting to be fed with rubble or whatever the occupants could find to burn.

"At least we're close to the toilets."

"Yes," said Oma, "I suppose that's something."

They stayed in the camp at Hannover for a while. How long, no one remembers. Time was suddenly unimportant. What mattered most was survival in a hostile world – food and shelter. Opa knew that they would have to move on, once they had gathered some strength again. There was no future for them here, sitting waiting for help to come to them. He believed that the future depended on choices you made and paths you trod. Admittedly you had to look at what was dished up to you and make the best of it.

Next it was more trains and sleeping on stations, sometimes only cups of tea as sustenance for the day, a mug of soup if you were lucky. Then walking through the countryside when there was neither train nor tracks. Sometimes their countrymen gave them food, potatoes, a piece of bread and maybe a bed in the barn. More often they were met with hostility. There were so many homeless people in desperate straits roaming from place to place. Farmers had to feed their own families and rooms in their homes were commandeered for refugee families. Even though they were not welcomed, occasionally they were able to work for a farmer in exchange for food and lodging.

CHAPTER ELEVEN

Slowly the winter passed and spring had arrived. The six Kliers stood on the bank of the Rhine. It was a cool morning but Opa wanted to be on the march early to get the ferry across the river. Rays of sun stretched sleepily, reluctant to rise over the horizon. There were other people there before them waiting for the ferryman to start work. Probably homeless like them, thought Oma, as she glanced at the disheveled and scrawny bunch. Dieter wandered along under the trees and bushes looking for violets. There were wild flowers in the pasture but he did not like the look of the cows there. Some of them had big sharp horns.

He took a fistful of violets to Oma.

"For you, Oma. Smell!"

"They're beautiful Dieterle," she smiled.

Today it seemed there was hope after all. Opa had heard that life was much better further west. There was only one way to find out. He hoped to get work there so that the family could stay in one place for a while. But first they must cross the Rhine. The punt was a large flat wooden platform, floating just above the water level. Along one side a metal cable snaked through rings on the edge of the punt to keep it from veering off downstream with the current. Ah, there was the ferryman, dressed in dull overalls with a hat pulled down over his face as if he had something to hide. Arm muscles bulged as he dug the pole into the river bed to move the barge slowly at first, then gradually faster as the punt eased its way across the river. His feet were planted firmly as he put his back into it. Dieter watched in awe from the safety of Oma's skirt. She tousled his hair and smiled.

"We're nearly there."

With a thump they arrived at the other bank. As they stepped onto dry land and headed up the bank Opa thanked the ferryman.

"Goodness knows how he makes a living now. Not many have money to pay for his services," Opa commented.

"Maybe he gets food from the farmers in return for a fare."

They set off along the dusty road. With so little energy they were thankful that there were no hills to climb. Oma held Dieter's hand as he walked by her side. The road wound around through clumps of trees dotted here and there. In the distance Opa pointed out a small village to his offspring.

"Maybe we find work and food there, ja?" Wherever there was a settlement there would be farms supporting it. They walked on in silence taking in the sights and sounds of the countryside. Birds were pecking for grubs and worms in the fields, heads cocked on one side listening, then a sudden jab for a morsel. If only life was that simple! Gradually the village came close and they could see smoke drifting from chimneys, chooks scratching in yards and vegetable patches. It looked promising.

The road skirted a stand of tall trees obscuring part of the view. As they rounded the bend an involuntary gasp of horror left Oma's lips. A man's body dangled from a rope on a gallows! His mouth grimaced with the brutality of his death. He swung ominously in the breeze oblivious to the horrific effect he had on the family. It appeared he had been left there as a warning to others. Opa turned the family round.

"I don't think this is a good place to visit."

"Why is the scarecrow up high like that?" a small voice asked.

"I think they're trying to scare off people too."

So back they went to the ferryman and across the river once more.

Opa knew they would have to find food and quickly. They had very little to eat yesterday morning, nothing since. Although their stomachs had shrunk since leaving Bruex they needed to maintain energy to keep walking. Heinz and Rudi never missed an opportunity to help themselves to food. Thank God for hungry teenage sons. Farm houses skirted the village.

"We need food. You wander on with Liesl and Dieter." Opa said.

Oma knew the routine. "Take care," she replied.

Opa, Rudi and Heinz fanned out in different directions, heading back towards the village. Oma took Dieter's hand and walked on. Liesel strode ahead looking for a spot to rest while Dieter and Oma followed. He liked having Oma all to himself for a while.

"Look Oma, the cows are resting. No milk for us today."

"No Liebchen. Maybe tonight." She hoped so. It pained her to see him so thin. He needed good food to grow but they had to take what they could get and there was never enough. She looked across to where the cows rested in the shade chewing their cuds. A stream meandered through their paddock. She did not like the idea of stealing food but they had to do it to survive. Dieter slipped his hand from hers to fossick on the roadside as he went. He found a stick and poked around in the grass under a tree.

"Here's a hole Oma. See! Any little people?" Oma looked at his discovery.

"Yes but they're sleeping now like the cows. Come along. We need to be further away before Opa comes back."

Although it did not matter if they dawdled at times, now they would need to put as much distance as possible between them and the farmer when he discovered the theft. Occasionally she glanced back but could see neither hide nor hair of her men. Ahead Dieter spotted Liesel resting under a tree. He ran up to her and told her about the hole. She listened with forbearance. All she could think about was food.

"Come we need to keep moving." Oma caught up with them and they set off once more, moving ahead in silence. Eventually they saw Opa and the boys hurrying as fast as their sagging energy allowed. They were not keeping to the road but cutting out the corners across country. As they approached Opa grinned and opened his coat. His arm inside the coat held a goose's beak shut, his other arm, clamped down firmly on the outside, limited any other action the goose thought of taking.

"Not bad! This'll fill a gap in our bellies." Oma patted his arm and smiled. Her men were safe.

"Thank you."

But for now they must keep moving as fast as possible. They would not stop to eat till evening. Then they hoped to find a farmhouse where they could exchange the goose for food they could eat on the march. Maybe they would be allowed to sleep in the barn too. They set off with a spring in their step and hope in their bellies. They had food for another day.

CHAPTER TWELVE

Usually the Klier family followed the crowds. There was a kind of comradeship in it but Opa was aware that in the end it was everyone for themselves. As they traveled he kept his ears tuned to what was going on around him. Sometimes there were rumours, sometimes there were facts. You had to keep your wits about you if you were going to survive. At first people complained about the lack of food and the endless walking. As time went on their stomachs shrank and they learned to conserve energy for the important tasks. Opa looked over at his wife, Ellie he called her. She never complained but trod doggedly on. God had been good to him when he gave him Ellie.

She was sitting on the station at Duesseldorf, a scarf covering her dark hair. They had been lucky to get space on the train to Duesseldorf and lucky that the rails were still intact by the look of the towns and countryside they had passed through. It was late afternoon. The spring sunshine was going down and a chill setting in. People huddled in groups, deathly quiet apart from the odd sniff or whimper. An old man disturbed the quiet with a racking cough that seemed intent on turning him inside out. The smell of unwashed bodies and clothes that could stand alone if ever the wearer took them off, had dispersed somewhat in the fresh air on the station. Everyone was in the same boat and did not seem to notice it any longer. It was all relative. The air was fresher than in the carriage but it was no longer what they used to call "fresh" air. A pall of smoke, destruction and decay lurked in all the cities they passed through. The density of it was in proportion to the amount of carnage in each place.

Opa, Heinz and Rudi waited in the queue for mugs of tea from the Red Cross.

Slowly the queue inched forward and at last it was their turn.

"Six mugs of tea please, one for the child." He thanked the woman. "What about trains from here?"

"None I'm afraid, the lines and bridges have been knocked out."

"So where to from here?"

"There is a refugee camp nearby if you need a rest. First corner on your left, down two blocks and turn right."

"Thank you."

They picked up two mugs each and wended their way through the crowd, trying not to spill a precious drop.

Oma looked up hopefully as they approached.

"No, we must press on and hope," was all he said.

Oma tested Dieter's mug of tea with her little finger and blew on it to cool it some more.

"Soon, Liebchen."

Opa and his two sons and daughter wrapped their hands around the mugs and took tentative sips. The warm, strong liquid slid down their parched throats and seemed to warm them from the inside out. Dieter watched Oma take several sips of her tea before offering Dieter his mug.

"Take care. It might still be hot." Dieter copied the others, wrapping his thin little fingers round the mug. As he raised it to his lips the reflection of the amber liquid shimmered in his eyes. He blew gently and then sipped. A satisfied "ah!" escaped his lips from time to time. Oma looked at Opa and they both smiled. The cup of tea offered a thin warmth but it was wonderful. Like hospitality in a desert. They returned the enamel mugs to the Red Cross ladies and followed the crowd that left the station.

By the looks of things they were all headed for the camp. First corner on the left, two blocks down and turn right. Craters full of scrap metal and shattered buildings were dotted around them. The enemy had targeted industrial areas and done a good job of it. They had heard reports that Dresden was worse than this. Balls of fire had completely wiped out every living thing after the bombs. It was hard to imagine what it must look like, this was bad enough. A crooked signpost on the corner pointed heavenward. Koenigs Allee, it said. A sparrow perched on it, flitting its tail this way and that, seemingly undecided as to which way it should go. It flew down and pecked at some grasses growing at the edge of the pavement.

"He wants more food," said Dieter.

"Yes, don't we all."

They came to the camp at last. As they wandered up and down the rows Heinz and Rudi darted in doors looking for space for the family.

"Here we are," called Rudi triumphantly as he ushered them in. They were a long way from the stove but with two hundred bodies generating warmth it probably would not matter. At least they had a bed and a roof over their heads. Another advantage was a row of long drop latrines and an ablution block nearby. Oma left the rest of the family guarding their space as she took Dieter over to get some of the grime off his face and hands. They had no soap and she used the hem of her skirt to dry his face afterwards. Then she attended to her own ablutions.

From experience they knew that it was too difficult to find food around a camp with such a huge population. They would sleep a night or two and then move on, out into the countryside again. It was further to walk this way but when the rail was out it was the best way to find food – away from the crowds. They hunkered down for the night on the wooden platforms. Dieter snuggled up to Oma and they helped to keep each other warm. Around them other families settled down. A baby cried as a mother rocked it in her arms shushing it gently. It was early in the evening but there was nothing else for it but to sleep on the space you had found or risk losing it. Further down the hut an old man was shaken by his cough. A young woman supported him as she encouraged him to take a sip of water. More seemed to escape his mouth and trickle off his beard. Eventually the coughing subsided and she laid him down to sleep.

Liesel lay awake long after the rest of her family slept. She listened to the snores, snuffles, coughs and muttering as sleepers rehearsed the trials of life on the move. She wondered when this would all end, the interminable wandering, constant hunger and nowhere to call your own. She thought of the family they had left behind and wondered if they were wandering in a different direction. Her eyes filled with tears which trickled over her cheeks as she gradually succumbed to sleep.

In the morning the light seemed to ripple along the bank of sleepers waking them as it went. People stretched, yawned, sat up and rubbed their eyes, however the mood took them. Quiet murmurings could be heard and babies whimpered for food. Opa liked to be away early and get on the road. Suddenly there was a wail from the far end of the hut. The young woman who had tended the old man was shaking him but he would never wake again.

"It is a mercy," said Oma as she moved down to comfort the woman. Opa followed, instructing Heinz to stay with the others in the meantime. Opa and another man picked up the deceased and carried him out to find a place to bury him. Oma brought the young woman along the hut and freed Heinz and Rudi to help their father. They used whatever came to hand in the rubble behind the camp to dig a makeshift grave. They carefully laid him in it and covered him with a thick blanket of earth. Then they made the sign of the cross and returned to the hut. A group of people had gathered round the young woman, trying to console her. Opa put his arm round Oma.

"We can't stay here forever. We need to move on."

She nodded in agreement as she took Dieter by the hand and helped him down the wooden step.

CHAPTER THIRTEEN

The pattern repeated itself – walking when there was no train, scrounging or stealing food, finding whatever shelter they could for the nights. The cities were bombed and desolate but still they were compelled to go and see if maybe there would be employment or accommodation, perhaps a train to somewhere else. Opa heard talk that the situation was better further south. The family had travelled northwest to Hannover, then southwest to Duesseldorf.

"I think we should walk through the countryside some more but keep the railway line in sight. What do you say?"

"I think you are right. If we have to walk we need more food."

"Yes that's why we travel this way. But I don't want to walk more than we must."

They headed south trudging, walking, plodding on. Cologne was no better than Duesseldorf.

"Look at that. The cathedral is ruined." No longer did the tall spires grace the skyline of the city. The architectural masterpiece that had taken six hundred years to build had been blown apart in a matter of seconds.

"More bombs!"

"Yes little man. Too many bombs."

In front of the cathedral a twisted panzer tank squatted on the road. The Rhine wandered slowly by as though in mourning.

"We'll need to walk further. There'll be no trains here. Pray God the rebuilding starts soon."

Oma could only nod. There was nothing to be said. So much destruction of people, livelihoods and buildings.

They left Cologne behind, like birds heading south for winter. Only winter was over and the family was not flying. Progress was slow but inexorably they moved closer to their sanctuary, a place to rebuild their nest. The Rhine led them further south. Opa endeavoured to keep it in sight as they wandered and foraged for food. He knew that major settlements clustered its banks. At last they came to Bonn. The mayhem was not so great here so they tracked down the station in the hope that they could rest from walking. The morning was warm for late spring and the sun shone down as they straggled along. Yes, trains were traveling from Bonn. Once again they joined the crowd waiting for a train.

"I'm glad we didn't spend the night here."

"Yes," Opa replied. "Everywhere we go there are crowds of homeless people like us."

"It's nice when we can be on our own."

"I look forward to having that permanently. That's what keeps me going."

It was no use asking when the next train was due. They came when they came. It was less than a year since the end of the bombings when the Allies had taken over. They hunkered down near the station wall and waited with everyone else. There was nothing to be said, nothing to do but wait. Some dozed, mothers scolded children, afraid of losing them, telling them to stay close. Heinz and Rudi headed off to see what information they could glean.

"You know where we are. Come back quickly when the train comes." Opa watched them wander along and find a veranda post to lean against, near a middle aged couple on their own.

"Where are you headed?" No use wasting words, Heinz thought.

"South. There's nowhere else to go."

"How far can we go by train?"

"Who knows!"

"As far as possible," put in his wife.

"Yes I'll be glad when we can settle somewhere."

Rudi nodded.

"It's been too long, hasn't it?

In the distance a train whistle wailed. Rudi and Heinz hurried back to their parents. Everyone looked along the track as they edged forward for a good position when the train arrived. You had to be quick and assertive because no doubt some would be left behind to wait for the next train. Opa had it down to a fine art. He went first, elbowing his way through with Oma and Dieter right behind. It was up to Heinz, Rudi and Liesel to follow closely and get themselves on board. So far they had always made it onto the same train. Today when the train sidled in and ground to a halt, the plan worked again. Oma sank onto a seat with a sigh. The train was dark and crowded with standing room only for the last people on board. The guard in a tattered uniform walked along the platform slamming the doors. There was no need to call, "All aboard. The train is now departing for Wherever." It went without saying. There were low murmurs from some and other people stared silently into space as the train began to pick up speed. As the train took them beyond Bonn Dieter settled down with his nose against the window. He could feel the vibration from the train on the track. Outside he watched the sunlight flicker through trees. He could almost smell the wildflowers and feel the grass between his toes. Oma watched him and then began to dream of better times. She looked at the temporary wooden bridges built by the US Army. Everything in life had become transitory. They needed a bridge built between their old life and the new. She woke from her reverie as a stand of trees cast their shadows across the train.

"Where do you think we will end up Pepi?"

"Let's see how far this train takes us."

"Yes I long to settle down, stay in one place."

"So do I. It is not good for any of us like this."

"But we are still together."

"Yes we've done the best we can."

"Sometimes it's better not to know what's up ahead, take life as it comes."

Opa smiled then.

"I'm relieved we didn't know about this. One day at a time, eh." He patted her hand.

Each of them sat nursing their thoughts. It was easier to talk when they were on the train. Walking required all their energy and they were constantly on the lookout for food. But for now they luxuriated in the train doing the hard grind for them.

Opa caught Oma's attention and nodded towards Dieter. The movement of the train had put him to sleep and his head slid down the window. Gently she put one hand under his head and tucked him under her arm. He never complained, just fossicked and chattered as they walked along. Sometimes he cried out in his sleep and she wondered what memories he was sifting through. Towards late afternoon the train slowed and came to a halt. Opa craned his neck to read the name of the station. Mannheim. They had done well to get this far but the lack of people on the station meant only one thing. This train was not going any further. Resignedly they climbed out and regrouped. Opa took Dieter by the hand as Oma set him down. They walked out following the crowd. Opa approached a family group.

"Where do we go from here? I'm new to these parts."

"Well I think Schweinfurt's the best bet from here. Although you never can tell."

"Why do you say Schweinfurt?"

"Maybe it's OK there. I heard Bavaria's not as badly hit as other places."

"Let's find out."

So Schweinfurt it was.

"At least we know where we're going this time."

Opa decided that they would travel cross country, almost due east for a while.

"If we have to walk let's take the shortest route."

They followed the banks of the Neckar River at first, where the villages and farms nestled. It was a long haul as they were not passing through any major towns and cities. There were no trains to catch but the serenity of the countryside and the warmer weather as spring turned into summer made up for that. Wildflowers bloomed and birds sang. There was reason to hope that life could be peaceful and fulfilling once more.

It took almost two weeks before they arrived at a town with a railway station - Bischofsheim. From here the trains were running to Schweinfurt, a man at the station told them.

"Well almost to Schweinfurt. The place is a mess. Bastards bombed the Kugelfischer factory and everything around it. Not just once. As often as they felt like it. Bastards!"

"Dreadful," said Opa, shaking his head as he moved away. He regretted bringing the family this way now but at least there was a train. It would speed things up and they could decide where to go next when they arrived.

It was hot on the train. If they opened the windows too far smuts from the smoke came in so they had to put up with it. At least this was a short ride compared to the trip from Bonn. The train stopped outside Schweinfurt. Heinz wound down the window and put his head out to see where they were.

"Careful son," cried Oma. They had gone through too much trouble and sorrow for it to end with Heinz getting his head stuck in a train window.

"There it is. I can see Schweinfurt ahead. Well, I guess it's Schweinfurt because I can see a fractured skyline."

They clambered down from the train and set off towards the city. It was just past noon and there was no shelter from the sun. Fortunately it was not far to walk. Opa and Oma looked at each other in despair as they walked into Schweinfurt. The glare of the sun on twisted metal hurt their eyes. The smell of smoke and decay enveloped them. What was that noise? Oma turned her head. It was the sound of loose sheet metal flapping against the skeleton of a building. Not even the sunshine could brighten up the carnage of the bombed ball-bearing factories.

"When will it end? How far has this devastation travelled?" Tears welled up in Oma's eyes. She'd hoped their wandering was almost over. Opa put his arm around her shoulders and hugged her to him. Dieter wound his arms round her legs and hugged her too.

"It's all right Oma. Nearly there." She smiled then and wiped her tears away with the back of her hand.

"Oh dear God! I'm sorry."

Once again Opa asked a group of people where they were going. It was the only way to find out. Sure, it was not always reliable but there had to be some place in all of Germany where they could settle. Please God, somewhere near here!

"We're heading south," said an older man. He clutched his jacket to his skinny frame with one hand as he pointed south. "Away from the industrial areas. They've been the worst hit."

"Sounds sensible to me," said Opa. "Thanks."

He hoped that this gentleman had his facts right. As they turned their backs on the horror of Schweinfurt to head on the road south new hope sprang up in him.

"Let's see where this leads," was all he said.

They stayed with the road, walking along the side. Trees offered shade once they had left the city well behind. Dieter walked with Rudi. Opa put his hand through Oma's arm and they walked in a companionable silence. His Ellie. He had wanted better for her than this. She never complained, always did what needed to be done. My word, as soon as possible, he would make it up to her. He did not know how, he did not know when. He just knew.

Suddenly he became aware of a low rumble creeping up from behind them. The others spun around too. A truck!

"Run!" Rudi tucked Dieter under his arm as they all ran behind the trees to hide. Dieter put his hands over his eyes.

"They can't see me now," he whispered.

"Ssh!" Oma beckoned for him to sit down beside her. A huge US Army truck rounded the bend and roared past.

"The Amerikaner are here too!"

"Did you see those huge wheels?"

When the dust settled they resumed their journey, looking for a likely place to sleep and maybe eat first.

CHAPTER FOURTEEN

Another city. Bamberg. Only now there was a difference. Hope lurched in their hearts as they looked around. It had been dashed so many times before. As they wandered by they stared at the buildings.
"Look Oma, no bombs here."
Oma hugged Dieter to her.
"No Dieterle. No more bombs!" She knew what they wanted, what they did not dare hope for. As they rounded each corner the buildings towered above them, standing proud and strong. Two-storeyed houses that had been there for hundreds of years still sheltered the generations living within the walls. Bright red geraniums burst from the window boxes in defiance it seemed. The cobbled streets were narrow but the sun shone above them. An old woman hurried along. She had a scarf tied firmly under her chin and carried a covered basket. Opa stopped her.
"Please tell me the way to City Hall."
She pointed with a crooked finger.
"Straight ahead for two blocks, left, then right, over the bridge and you're there."
"Thank you."
She nodded and hurried along again. She had somewhere to go, where she belonged. With a wistful sigh Oma followed her family.
"Look there it is." They turned the final corner and the river sparkled in the sunlight. A barge crept under the bridge, intent on not disturbing the peaceful scene it seemed.
A queue snaked along the footpath, straggling over the bridge. The Kliers sheltered from the sunshine in the shade of the building.
"Can I see the barge?" Rudi took Dieter by the hand and lead him to the bridge. He hoisted Dieter onto his back so that he could see over the solid stonework.
"It's going slowly but it's nearly gone."

"Yes Dieter, just moving slowly but it gets there."

"Where is it going?"

"I don't know but the captain does."

"Where are we going Rudi?"

"I don't know."

"We need a captain too."

"Yes we need a captain. Maybe Opa will find out soon where we can go."

"He can be the captain then."

Rudi smiled as they rejoined the family. A sparrow perched on a signpost, flitting first this way then that, keeping an eye out for something to eat. It flew down hopefully as a mother took out a hunk of dark bread and fed it piece by piece to a toddler. She wouldn't drop a crumb if she could help it. The sparrow hopped around, a safe distance away, cocking its head from side to side. The mother shooed it away if it came too close. Food was precious, easier for birds to find than people. Slowly the queue wound forward. Opa watched the people who came out of the Accommodation Bureau, talking urgently to each other, intent as though they had a purpose in life again. Could he hope again? He thought this could be an end to their wandering.

At last it was Opa's turn. He opened the carved wooden door of City Hall and walked in. He was not dressed for the occasion. He smiled to himself. How far they had come, travelling kilometers, but also away from many things that he used to think were 'proper,' the only way they should be done. Oh well, his pride had been left behind long ago. The middle aged man looked over the top of his glasses as Opa approached. Everything here was so neat and orderly that he felt he was in a different world.

"Accommodation please! My family needs accommodation. And work. I'm a good worker." It all tumbled out, not the way Opa had intended. The man held up his hand.

"Excuse me but I cannot help. I am sorry but Bamberg is too full now. There is no more accommodation here."

Opa's shoulders slumped as he asked in a desperate voice, "But what do I do? We have come so far. Where can we go?"

The official softened his stance a little. "I am sorry sir. I understand. Go to Ebern. They can help you there."

"Where is Ebern? Must we walk again?"

"No, there are trains. It's about twenty-five kilometers north of here. Go to the Accommodation Bureau in Ebern. I'm sure they can help you there."

"Thank you." He must be polite in spite of his huge disappointment. Opa turned his back on the man behind the desk and trudged back past the hopeful people still waiting.

"Come," was all he said to the family as they headed off back the way they had come. Once they were round the corner Oma grabbed his arm.

"Tell me, Peppi!"

"There's nothing here. Full house. We're on the road again. To Ebern. Not far. On the train tomorrow. Camp here tonight." He spoke in short sentences not daring to say too much, trying to control his voice.

"Let's go then."

Another night in a refugee camp like sardines in a tin, only the stink was worse. At first light they were up and off to the station. Stomachs rumbled but it did not seem to matter. What mattered was getting to Ebern as soon as possible before all the rooms were taken. They were tired, undernourished and dispirited. They knew they could not keep going much longer. The problem was there were thousands of others like them. If only today would be the end of their wandering. If only!

CHAPTER FIFTEEN

In Ebern they located the Displaced Persons' Office with little trouble. They looked for a queue. Opa waited on a roller coaster of emotions as the line inched forward. Dare he hope to start a new life? Was that too much to ask? Would they be disappointed again? So close but not close enough? They were moving slowly.

"Once you're registered here you'll be right," assured the man in front of them.

"Then you can go to the Accommodation Bureau and the Employment Office."

Opa met Oma's gaze. No words were spoken but a spark of hope was kindled there. At last it was their turn. An official directed them to a desk by the window. Here they were interviewed by a man in a worn brown suit. Obviously he had not suffered the effects of war like some. He wrote down their particulars – full name, date and place of birth, relationships and last address. He showed no surprise, no emotion as they recounted their journey out of Sudetenland and around war torn Germany. He took ID cards from his desk and inserted one in his typewriter. Painstakingly, slowly he typed out cards for each one, with Dieter's name on Oma's card. He stamped each of them with a thump and handed them to Opa.

"Now go to the Accommodation Bureau in the next street. They will help you further."

"Thank you!" It felt amazing to be an officially recognised citizen again, not a pawn in someone's war games. They looked hopefully from one to the other.

"That's a good start."

"Now for somewhere to live."

"Can I have a real bed Oma?"

"Wait and see. I think so."

At the Accommodation Bureau there was another queue, not any longer than before because they could move no faster than the officials could deal with applications. Oma was pleased they had started out early. There was much to be done today. The officer checked their IDs and noted the size of the family. Then he riffled through a folder on his desk.

"Here we are, Herr Klier. We have a room for you with a farmer at Zaugendorf. Dirauf's the name."

He wrote their names and the address onto their accommodation papers and stamped it with a rubber stamp. It was official. They had somewhere to live.

"But first you must go to the Employment Office. They will give you work."

It gets better and better thought Heinz. He was looking forward to a decent meal every day.

"Here is an allowance in the meantime to pay your first rent and buy some food."

"Thank you, sir!" Opa bowed as he took the coupons and carefully stowed them in the inside pocket of his jacket with the ID cards. Like gold!

Now to the Employment Office. Oma, Liesl and Dieter sat in a waiting room while Opa, Heinz and Rudi went into the office.

"I'm hungry Oma."

"I know Dieter. We must wait for Opa and the boys then we'll get food."

Dieter slid off his chair and went over to the window. He could see everyone outside still waiting. He waved to a little girl but she just looked away. He looked out across the cityscape, tall trees, buildings, breathing in the fresh air. No smell of smoke to choke the senses. Peace. Oma settled into her chair in a reverie, her mind taking her back to her home in Bruex. She wondered where the rest of the family was now. They had their plans too and she hoped it had worked out well for them. The older folk would not have survived the torturous journey they had been on.

More women and children joined them in the waiting room. It became hot and stuffy. She joined Dieter by the window, hoping for some fresh air but there was no breeze. She felt sure that the length of time the men were taking was a good sign. "No" was a quick response. To organise work took longer. From time to time she glanced at the door.

"Look Oma. See the church spire. It's pointing to God."

"Yes Dieter. God is here too."

He took her hand and leant against her skirt. Oma was his security blanket.

"Ellie." She turned to see Opa beckoning from the doorway. "Come!" He was smiling and so were the boys. Oma and Dieter sidled through the room full of people.

"Yes?"

"We have work. The three of us. In Bamberg at the US Army stores."

"Is it far from Zaugendorf?"

"No, there are trains."

"Thank God! Let's go. Where can we find food?"

"There will be some nearby."

CHAPTER SIXTEEN

It was late afternoon by the time they reached Zaugendorf. The sun smiled down on the family as they walked across the bridge over the River Itz. Birds sang in the poplars lining the bank. The Klier family looked at the farmhouse that was to be their home. It was a solid structure. A concrete path with a ramp led to the front door. The walls were roughcast painted with lime. The gabled roof with terracotta tiles was dotted with dormer windows to let light into the upstairs rooms. The windows peeped out like children watching the family's approach. A dog stood guard by its kennel, paws planted apart, barking loudly. An ample busted woman opened the front door. She wiped her hands on her apron as she surveyed the scraggly bunch.

"Yes, can I help?"

Opa fished in his pockets for the papers.

"Frau Dirauf?" She nodded as her heart sank. She had dreaded this moment. Her husband was angry to think that their home could be taken over by the authorities like this.

"Josef Klier is my name. We have been sent here by the Accommodation Bureau." He paused. It was hard for him too. They had been forced out of their own home and had to flee. About a year ago but it seemed so much longer.

"Wait please. My husband's in the stable." She scurried away. Shortly her husband appeared. He was a tall, well muscled man, used to hard work. His mouth was set in a firm line.

"Dirauf's the name."

"Josef Klier, my wife Elisabeth, our children Heinz, Rudi and Liesl and grandson Dieter." He paused not sure of their welcome. Tentatively he held out their papers. Drat the man! Didn't he realise what it was like to be kicked out from home and country to wander around as unwanted pests.

Dirauf harumphed as he handed the papers back.

"Come." He opened the door and beckoned to his wife. "Mari will help you."

"Thank you," Opa said to his retreating back.

Mari appeared to relax a little now. She hoped the worst was over and they could live peaceably together at least. She welcomed them with a smile now.

"Come I will show you to your room." Six of them! She'd hoped for a smaller family. But my word they were so thin. She led them down the hallway. Dieter's eyes were wide as he looked through an open door on the right into the kitchen. By the doorway stood a dresser with cupboards underneath and shelves with plates, bowls and cups. An elderly woman was setting a large table ready for their evening meal. A plump little girl toddled along behind her. The smells emanating from the stove made his stomach rumble.

The hallway turned left and Mari ushered them into a room. It was shady at this time of day but a window looked out on the poplars and river at the front of the house. An army bed was placed under the window and a plain wooden table pushed up to it. Four chairs were scattered round the table. A stout iron stove stood against the wall with a kettle waiting nearby. A double bed was squeezed into the corner near the table and another in the opposite corner with a chest of drawers in between. They surveyed the room each thinking their own thoughts. It would be very cramped.

"The toilet?" asked Oma. Dieter was bound to ask for that soon. Mari pointed out the door and then left towards the end of the passage.

"Come." The entourage followed and she showed them the toilet. A large wooden seat was built from wall to wall with a wooden lid above a long drop. A window stood open to let in fresh air. She shut the door again and latched the hook.

"And here the big boys can sleep."

Oma breathed a sigh of relief as Mari opened a door on the other side of the toilet. Sun shone through a small window lighting up a tall wardrobe and bunks squeezed into a tiny bedroom.

"Thank you. You are most kind," Oma said.

Mari smiled and nodded as she took her leave and hustled back to attend to her crying daughter. She would not like to be squashed into such a small area but then by all accounts it was much better than anything they had had for quite some time. Poor things!

Opa lit the fire in the stove and sat at the table watching while Oma set out plates and cups. She opened cupboard doors and found cutlery and a teapot.

"Ah that's good." Then she cut the bread into thick slices and some of the cheese too. Heinz and Rudi wandered in from their room. It hadn't taken them long to put their meager belongings into the wardrobe.

Dieter sidled out and leant on the door frame leading into Dirauf's kitchen. The old grandmother was sitting near the stove with the little child on her knee.

"Come here," she said beckoning to Dieter. Hesitantly he moved further into the room looking behind him.

"Come, little one."

"He is so thin! Give him some milk."

Mari poured some milk into a pitcher. Just then Rudi came looking for him.

"This is for the child," she said and passed it to Rudi.

"Say thank you to Frau Dirauf, Dieter."

"Thank you, kind lady."

At long last the day was over and what a day it had been. Everyone was in bed, the boys in their bedroom, Liesl and Dieter in one double bed, Oma and Opa in the other.

"Well a house to live in at last."

"Yes and a job to go to tomorrow and food."

"Oh Josef, it's been so long. I'd almost given up hope."

"I know. This is only the beginning of our new life. I want more for you than this. I don't know how we will do it but I will build you a home. I promise."

"Oh Peppi," was all she could say as they settled down for their first night in accommodation that was theirs for as long as they needed it.

CHAPTER SEVENTEEN

It was a sunny day. Just right for doing the washing. Oma set to early with Liesel's help carting buckets of water from the river. A large cauldron sat on the stove and steam began to rise from it. There Oma boiled up the whites with soap powder. It was hot work as she stirred the washing with a thick stick. She brushed a loose strand of hair aside and tucked it behind her ear. Now Liesel was tipping cold water into the tin bath on the floor. That was where Oma rinsed the washing before spreading it over the bushes to dry.

"Oma, where can I go today?"

"We're not going anywhere. Can't you see I've got washing to do? You just run along and play."

Dieter walked outside thinking. Oma would be busy most of the day. Outside Luchs gave a half-hearted "Woof" that asked "Are you going to play with me today?" But Dieter could see that Luchs was on his chain and he was not allowed to let him off.

"No Luchs, not just now. Maybe later." He patted his head and wandered off. Ahead he saw a cluster of cornflowers growing at the edge of the pasture. I know, he said to himself, I'll go and visit God and take him some flowers. He picked a bunch of cornflowers and looked around for poppies to brighten the bunch. He remembered he had seen some in the meadow up behind the house. Oma would be pleased with his good idea. She always said, 'Oh dear God.' Often Dieter had watched out the window as villagers walked past going to church. One day he had gone with Mari Dirauf and Johanna.

"Now you must sit quietly. This is God's house," she'd told him.

He could go to God's house on his own. He would love to have a good look around but be quiet if that was the way God liked it. Now he had a lovely bunch of flowers. He wandered down through the village very happy with himself. As he approached the little stone church he noticed the door was shut. Oh well, he would just have to knock. He climbed up the steps and knocked. He heard it echo through the church but no one came to the door. He waited and then decided to try the door. With all his might he tried to turn the knob but it was firmly locked. Dieter sat down on the step and scratched his head. What should he do with the beautiful flowers? It seemed a shame to just leave them on the doorstep and anyway God would not know who they were from.

As he walked slowly back the way he had come he saw an old lady sweeping her front step and along the path with a straw broom. She gave him a smile and a wave. He could always get some more flowers for God. He walked towards her and held out the flowers.
"I picked these for God but he's not at home so you can have them."
"Why thank you. You are so sweet."

It seemed as though the little church in Zaugendorf was always locked except when Mass was being held. When Oma and Opa went to Muersbach, he often ran ahead to run his hands over the huge stone cross by the path. In the church he had seen Jesus on the cross and wondered who had done that to him. There was so much that he did not understand in his world. He knew that planes used to fly over and drop bombs. He knew that soldiers had come and taken their home and their family had been torn apart. He knew that they had often been hungry and sometimes Oma cried. But he did not know why. Not that he blamed God. Oma called him 'dear God' so obviously it was not his fault. Anyway people had done bad things to God too. He really should take him some more flowers. If he could not catch him in his house in Zaugendorf then he would just have to go to Muersbach. The church door was always open there. He had seen it.

So one day when Oma was busy Dieter set off on his own. It was a mile to Muersbach but he sang to himself as he stooped to pick flowers. He picked a large bunch this time because God's house in Muersbach was much bigger. Yes, he was home. The front door was open and the sun streamed onto the black and white tiles. He stood inside the door and looked around. He was pleased he had come. It seemed as though God was beckoning him. So softly, quietly he made his way up to the altar. A red light flickered in a lantern on the wall beside the altar. As he became accustomed to the dim light his eyes travelled round the sanctuary. Everything about this place was beautiful and peaceful. Thank goodness the soldiers had not come to throw God out. Where would he find another house like this?

Dieter climbed up the steps to the altar to put the flowers there. He stood on tiptoes and reached up but he could not quite make it. He looked around but he did not think he should stand on the red velvet seats. He could not do that with his shoes on. Then again he did not want to leave the flowers on the floor because someone might walk on them. He spotted the side altar. It was beautiful too. Maybe he could reach that. Yes, he could. Carefully he placed the bunch on the table and turned them round so you could see them from the door.

"Dear God, these are for you." He kissed his hand and placed it on the flowers. God had some flowers from him at last.

CHAPTER EIGHTEEN

It was winter in 1946. Darkness came earlier now. There had been no snow but it was so cold that they knew it was just around the corner. Life was more predictable and the family had settled into a comfortable routine. The men were home from work and Opa was reading the news from the paper he brought home every day – the Frankischer Tag. A single light in the middle of the room tried valiantly to keep the darkness at bay. Dieter was playing on the floor between the beds. He used twigs, pebbles and his imagination to make something out of nothing. Oma stood at the stove stirring the soup as she plopped in the dumplings. Mmmm it smelled good, onions, parsley, a soup bone and she had even managed to get a small amount of meat from trading socks on the black market.

"Soup's ready soon." She could almost hear the boys' stomachs rumbling but they knew better than to hustle her.

"Set the table please Liesel."

Just then there was a knock at the door. Now that was strange, no one knocked at the door at this time of day. Opa looked at Oma, puzzled, as he crossed the room and opened the door.

"My ....Come in, come in."

Oma dropped the ladle into the soup with a splash.

"Soukob," she screamed. "Is it really you?" She wiped her hands on her apron and hugged him, crying.

"Where have you......?" She stopped short. She guessed where he had been, Soukob and his family. He was so thin and gaunt, no longer tall and straight but stooped. He took off his hat and rubbed a hand over his bald head.

"Is it really you?"

Opa pulled a chair out for him to sit down.

"We're just about to eat. You're just in time. Another place, Liesel."

"Please Josef, first you must take down the light shade. We need to celebrate."

"How can we celebrate with a light shade?"

"I have eggs. I must make a cake in it."

Opa smiled as he placed a chair underneath the light. Oma opened the door on the stove to let out a glow as Rudi turned off the light. Opa handed the shade to Oma. The only problem was the hole in the middle but he knew his Eli had something in mind. Deftly she cleaned the shade, dried it and placed a larger circle of paper over the hole. She stoked the fire some more and shut the door.

"Now for a cake." Dieter watched as she beat eggs and sugar with a wooden spoon in a bowl. Her arm went so fast as she held the bowl against her chest. She lifted the spoon above the bowl and watched the thick creamy mixture slowly fall back in a stream. Yes it was just right. She added a pinch of salt and some milk and stirred some more. Next she added flour and gently folded it in. Carefully she spooned it into the improvised cake pan making sure the paper stayed in place.

"Now into the oven with it and we can eat our soup."

Oma looked at the back of this man. She felt a sense of dread in the pit of her stomach. She knew that his wife and children were dead. This Jewish family had disappeared from Bruex overnight and they had feared the worst. Liesel handed the bowls to Oma as she ladled the soup into them. Then she took them to the table.

"Gee, this smells good." Rudi did not begrudge sharing it with a family friend but it was difficult for a hungry young man to wait the extra time.

Soukob took his time, eating slowly and savouring each mouthful. His hand trembled as he lifted the spoon to his mouth.

"I thought I would never get to eat another meal with you," he said.

"We thought the same. How did you find us?"

"When I was released from the labour camp we were taken to the Search Office at the Red Cross." He stared at his bowl blinking. "I wanted to find out about my wife and children. But it was too late for them. We were separated, sent to different camps and now…." he gulped back a sob, "they are gone forever."

"Such a shock for you. I am sorry." Opa comforted him with a hand on his shoulder. Oma hastened to check the cake in the oven, wiping her eyes on the corner of her apron.

"Not ready yet. Would you like more soup?"

"Just a little please." Then he continued. "The Search Office told me that many Sudetendeutsche had settled around this area so once I had my ID card I could travel. And so here I am. It was easy to find you through the Accommodation Bureau. I just hoped you'd made it."

There was a long pause. Yes they had made it! Opa looked at his family. They had lost everything but they still had each other. That was what really mattered. The deprivation they had gone through was nothing compared to Soukob's hell. He looked around the room. They had shelter, warmth, light, food and family compared to the darkness and chill that had invaded his friend's heart and soul. Opa shuddered as he pondered the loneliness and despair Soukob must be enduring.

"You poor man."

"And what about you? How did you get here?"

"Well we went the long way round in a huge circle. We just had to follow the crowds. There was no accurate information."

"I understand. Relying on hearsay is like being on a rollercoaster that doesn't stop for you to get off."

"Sometimes we got a train but many times we had to walk - over the Ore Mountains, across to Hannover, down to Duesseldorf then Wiesbaden, Schweinfurt, Bamberg, Ebern and finally here. Always hoping that one day the wandering would finish."

Soukob nodded. Oma checked the cake once more. Yes it was golden and cooked to perfection. She took the pan out and set it on the side to cool. From the kitchen dresser she took down the jar of roasted acorns and chickory and poured some into the coffee grinder. Holding the grinder against her belly she turned the handle until it was all ground. She set the coffee pot underneath and let the grounds patter into the pot. Next she took it over to the stove, poured in boiling water from the kettle, gave it a quick stir and left it to brew. She turned the cake out onto a plate and dusted it with a little of her special icing sugar.

"Cups and plates please Liesel." Oma cut slices of cake and set the plate in the middle of the table with a jug of milk and saccharine tablets. Sugar came mixed with semolina so that it could only be used for baking. It did not go well in coffee. While Liesel poured the coffee, Oma handed out the cake. Dieter watched her every move, waiting for his plate. The smell was enough to drive him crazy. It had been a long time since they had had cake.

"Erika is not with you. And what about your brother Franz?" Soukob asked Oma as she poured him some more coffee.

"Erika met us on the station in Chemnitz so we know she got out alive. She lives her own life and could be anywhere now. Josef tracked down Franz and Else for me. They are living in Trauenstein near Munich. They are both well."

"I must visit them soon."

"Yes but you must stay here tonight. It is too late to go back to your lodgings now."

"That is very kind."

"We have the army bed here."

"I am used to sleeping anywhere. It will be warm by the stove."

As Opa explained how to get to Trauenstein by train Oma and Liesel cleared the table and washed the dishes in the enamel bowl on the end of the table. Rudi and Heinz excused themselves and went to bed. They started out early each morning for work in Bamberg. Oma noticed Dieter beginning to droop.

"Bed for you too, Dieterle."

Dieter slid off his seat and walked around to Soukob. Although it had been a time to celebrate he sensed that Soukob was very sad. Dieter stood beside him with a hand on his knee.

"Good night. Have a good sleep."

"Good night my boy," Soukob responded.

The next day Opa took Soukob to the train and bought him a ticket. He would do anything for his friend. It was good that he could visit Franz again. They had been close friends in Bruex after all. Franz and Else helped Soukob find accommodation in Trauenstein but the hardships of life in a camp and the loss of his loved ones had left its indelible mark. A few months later Opa visited him and realized that he was very sick. He took Soukob to hospital where he died a few days later. No one knew the cause of death but Oma suspected it was a broken heart.

CHAPTER NINETEEN

At last it was Christmas Eve. Dieter had helped Oma prepare. They had cleaned and scrubbed.

"Is that good Oma?"

"Yes love. You are a very good sweeper."

Oma had cut fresh paper to line the dresser shelves with a fancy edge hanging down the front. Then they made snowflake decorations.

"I like this one." Dieter dabbed some flour and water paste onto it.

"Not too much Dieter. It'll ooze out on the windows and won't look nice."

He scraped some off with the spoon and stuck it to the window. Some more snowflakes went up on the door. Opa had cut small pine branches on his way home from work the night before. Liesel took a chair over to the door.

"Hand me a pine branch please."

Dieter rushed over to help as Liesel attached pine branches over the lintel. Gradually they worked their way round the room till all the branches were used – on shelves, along the window sill, over the holy picture above Oma and Opa's bed.

"Let's use this big one for our Christmas tree. But we'll need more decorations."

"I'll help." Dieter moved over to the table where there was more white paper and a little bit of foil from the chocolate bars that Opa managed to find at the army base. With painstaking care it had been turned into tinsel. Liesel made an angel for the top of the tree.

"I'll make stars and snowflakes. I'm good at those." Away he went, folding the paper then snipping pieces out. His jaw worked up and down in time with the scissors. His concentration was deep, no time for talking now. Finally they stood back to survey their masterpiece.

"How does that look Mama?"

"Wonderful. I think you've done very well."

Last year no one knew it was Christmas. They had been walking, wandering, far from any place they could call home. Opa and the boys were outside chopping firewood that they brought home from the forest. Dieter heard someone stomping in from the stable.

"Door!" called Rudi. Dieter opened the door to let Rudi in with an armful of wood.

"That's your job, Sonny. You're the door man. You can open and shut the door for me."

Rudi stacked the wood at the side of the stove and went out for more. They needed plenty to keep themselves warm and cook their Christmas meal. It was beginning to snow again and soon it would be dark.

Oma had crumbed the fish. A cake was cooling in the upturned light shade on the dresser. Dieter's fingers twitched as he looked at it. He grasped them behind his back so they would not cause trouble for him by picking at it.

"Set the table please Liesel." Oma opened the oven door and looked in the pan. The fish was almost cooked. Good! Just then Opa came in rubbing his hands and blowing on them.

"Temperature's dropping out there and it's snowing again."

"Dinner's nearly ready."

"Mmmm, smells delicious."

Dieter had sidled in behind the curtain by the window. He looked at the icicles forming on the outside and the real snowflakes to match his cutouts. Light from the room shone on a patch of snow in front of him. He touched the window with a finger. How cold the glass was. No wonder the storks flew south for the cold months.

"Opa, see what I made."

"Who's that?"

A smiling face peeped out from behind the curtain.

"Oh, it's you. You'd better show me what you've been up to."

"Look! Snowflakes! I folded the paper and cut tiny pieces out. Aren't they pretty?"

"Yes they are." Opa smiled. "It's a wonder they don't melt."

"They're made of paper, Opa."

If only life was that simple, Opa mused. Cut it out to suit yourself. Make it how you want it. For them everything had flipped out of control but maybe this year.....

"I'm watching for the Christ child."

Opa was brought back to the present.

"Are you now? Let me know if you see him. I've got a job to do." He sidled out as Dieter started singing to himself.

"Oh Christmas tree, oh Christmas tree, how brightly gleam your branches."

Opa placed a gift under the Christmas tree in the corner. There was only one this year – a pair of slippers for Dieter. He looked at Ellie and smiled.

"Are you hungry Dieter?" Oma called.

"Yes very."

"Well dinner's ready."

Dieter fought his way out from behind the curtain.

"I think the Christ child must have come through the stable. See!" Opa pointed to the Christmas tree. Dieter's face lit up.

"Wow, are they for me?"

"Well, let me see. Do they fit Oma?"

"They're for me!" Dieter swooped on the brown slippers. Real slippers. He sat on the floor, pushed his stockinged feet into them and fastened the buttons.

"They're just right. Look Oma, Opa." He stood up and walked up and down wiggling his toes in the warmth and snugness against his feet.

"They're very smart slippers. Mind you, they're just for inside. You never wear slippers outside or your feet would get wet and cold."

"Yes Oma."

"Up to the table, time for dinner."

"Can I leave my slippers on?"

"Of course, silly!" Heinz got up from his seat in the corner. He was keen to eat.

Oma served spoonfuls of potato salad onto the plates and then slid crumbed fillets of fish beside it. Carp was all she could get this year. She carefully removed the bones from Dieter's fish.

"Watch out for bones! There could be more."

Opa looked at his plate. It never ceased to amaze him how Elly could get what she needed to make a delicious meal.

"Gherkins! We even have gherkins."

"Yes, Mrs Fischer had two extras." Oma smiled.

Hard-boiled egg, cubed potatoes, grated onion and gherkin all tossed in farm fresh cream. He felt sure this year would be better. Later they finished their Christmas meal with coffee and cake sprinkled with cinnamon and icing sugar. Oma and Liesel had cleaned up and done the dishes. Dieter was curled up fast asleep in bed with his slippers by his side. The rest of the family drew chairs up to the stove and opened the oven and firebox doors.

"I wonder how Franz and Else are tonight?" Oma often wondered how her brother and sister in law were faring and if they were well.

"Yes, I'm thinking of the rest of our family too."

"We must visit them sometime. Do you think we could?"

"Who knows? There's so much we still have to do."

"All in good time. It's good that we've got each other." They looked at their three grown children.

"It'll be better when we have our own house again. More room," Rudi added.

"Yes, I can't wait." Liesel was looking forward to having her own bed at least, rather than having to share it with a little nephew.

"We're working on it but it won't be next year," Opa replied.

Oma reached over and patted Opa's knee.

"I appreciate all the hard work my three men are doing."

"We get any extras we can, too," Heinz said with a grin.

"Yes but we must always be careful."

CHAPTER TWENTY

Summer had come to Zaugendorf. Oma wiped a weary hand over her brow as she moved a pot of potatoes to the side of the stove. These days she looked forward to the cool of the evening but first she must finish preparing the meal for her men who had just come in from work. The sun had long since moved across the sky and the room was dim. A single light in the middle of the room shone valiantly on the homely scene. Oma set a pan to sizzle on the stove and dropped in chopped bacon. It was not often that she managed to get bacon for the roux sauce.

"Smells good!" Liesel was setting the table.

"Won't be long now."

Dieter lay on the floor on his tummy reading the paper. "What does this word say? E..f..f..i..g..y."

"Effigy," said Liesel.

"What's an effigy?" It was part of a frequent routine. Opa came in and left his paper on the table while he went to chop firewood. Dieter pounced on it and with Liesel's help had learned to sound out words and ask Oma or Liesel for help. He was reading remarkably well now, especially for a four year old.

"It's a dummy made to look like a real person."

"Oh!" Dieter continued reading in his painstaking way. A frown appeared. It was worrying news today.

Just then Opa came in and washed his face and hands in the bowl. He dried himself on the towel.

"It's hot out there."

"Yes it's been hot all day."

Opa moved over to the table. "What's this then! My paper's a mess."

Dieter scampered to make room for Opa.

"Why are they carrying pretend people in coffins through Bamberg streets?"

"They're angry with the government."

"They won't hurt people will they?"

Opa looked up from straightening his paper.

"How do you know about this?"

"I was just reading till you came in."

Opa looked from Oma to Liesel.

"How long has this been going on?"

"For a while. I've been teaching him his letters," Liesel said proudly.

"Come here." Dieter walked over to Opa looking at the floor.

"Can you read this to me?"

Dieter started, "Many p…p..e…people g..a…th…er…ed, gathered in Bamberg to…day."

"Well done! He's reading."

"Yes we know."

Opa thumped the table. Dieter jumped.

"Then why isn't he at school? A child who can read like that should be in school."

"Do you think they'd take him? He's only four and a half."

"Well let's ask. Then we'll know."

"I suppose so."

"Can I go to school? Please can I go to school?" Dieter was jumping up and down, his eyes bigger and rounder than usual in his excitement.

"We will see Dieterle. But now it's time to wash your hands for dinner."

The meal seemed like a celebration. What would have been an ordinary meal of potatoes in roux sauce was made special with the crispy bits of bacon and Dieter's excitement. His heart was singing as he prepared for bed later that evening. School! A big school boy like the others in the village. He didn't need to be coerced to go to bed but clambered in with a quick "goodnight" over his shoulder. He was a school boy now after all.

"What about Luchs? Aren't you going to say goodnight to him too?"

Dieter got out of bed and went to the window. He could just see two paws and a nose poking out of the kennel.

"I'll just say it from here. It's a bit dark."

"What's the problem all of a sudden?" Rudi asked.

"You never know who's out there! Goodnight Luchs. See you in the morning." He might be a big school boy but he did not want to take any risks after what he had read in the paper. He climbed back into bed, pleased that he made the right decision.

"My newspaper is for adults, not children," murmured Opa under his breath.

It was summer holidays when Oma prepared for Dieter to start school in July. She took Dieter to Muersbach and the teacher agreed that he was ready to begin his formal learning. She was young and pretty and she smiled at him as he finished reading to her. Her name was Miss Marianne.

"See you next week then."

"Yes we will." Oma took Dieter's hand as they walked home again along the path through the fields and meadows. He chattered without let-up leaving Oma in no doubt that school would be good for both of them. She loved her little grandson but wondered when his mother would claim him. School would allow him to play with other children his own age instead of spending most of his time with adults. Yes, Peppi was right.

At last the day dawned. Dieter was up and dressed before the thrushes and blackbirds had finished their morning song. Khaki shorts and a striped short-sleeved shirt, both made by Oma, with roman sandals on his feet. He looked at his school bag hanging on the end of the bed. Too early to put that on, but he'd packed it himself last night. It held a slate with a cloth and a sponge attached on the end of a string, a wooden box holding two slate pencils, as well as a wonderful army canteen with plate, cup and a knife, fork and spoon that clipped together. It was one of Opa's acquisitions especially for school. He felt like the luckiest boy in the world. After breakfast he scrubbed his face clean and Oma slicked his hair back with water on the comb. Then they set off for Muersbach and school. The two and a half kilometers seemed to fly by as Dieter skipped along at Oma's side.

The school was situated on the top floor of a three storeyed building with a tiled roof. It was an impressive structure built in the sixteenth century, probably the home of an obscure aristocrat. Since being converted to a school several generations of village children had been educated there. The ground floor was built of sturdy granite with a saddler at the far end. The first floor housed the saddler and his family above the shop. Next door were the school toilets, boys' and girls' on opposite sides of the stairs. Thank goodness for stout mud brick walls! Strong oak beams spanned each floor, filled in with mud brick and then rendered and painted with whitewash. Age-blackened timber strips outlined the panels.

Oma and Dieter wound their way up the stone stairs. Dieter was breathless after skipping along and climbing upstairs, as well as the excitement of the day. Oma smiled affectionately.

"A big school boy today!" He wondered why they called him big. He did not feel any bigger than yesterday but it was good not to be considered a baby anymore. Dieter caught his breath as Oma opened the door. They walked in. There were children everywhere. Bigger children were getting organised near the door at the back of the room. Along the side that faced the street there were three large windows where sunlight streamed in. Banks of desks stood in rows with an aisle down the middle of the room and one at each side. Dieter and Oma sidled past the clusters of children. Where was Fraulein Marianne? Dieter looked around. As a group of children moved aside he saw her, smiling a welcome. She stood in front of a large desk. Beside her was a stove to ward off winter's chills.

"Ah Frau Klier and Dieter. Welcome to our school." Fraulein held out her hand to Dieter. "Come and I'll show you to your desk." She led him over to the front row.

"Well, look at that! A desk to keep your things in." Oma lifted the lid and Fraulein indicated the space for his school essentials. A shelf ran along under the hinged desk top and already there were two other sets of belongings neatly stacked there.

"This is Helmut. He's sitting next to you with Olga on the end."
Helmut gave him a shy smile.

"Well that's about all you need to know just now. You'll soon get the hang of things."

Oma bent down to give Dieter a kiss. "I'll see you after school," she said.

Dieter had not realised Oma would leave so soon. Suddenly he did not feel quite up to the task of becoming a "big school boy." His eyes filled with tears and overflowed as he grasped Oma's skirt for comfort.

"He'll be all right," Fraulein reassured her.

"Yes. I'll see you after school. He's coming home with the other children from Zaugendorf," Oma added.

He gave a little cry as Oma prised her skirt from his hand and left the classroom.

"You come and stand next to Helmut. There you are." The teacher reached over and rang a bell on her desk. Silence descended like a cloak suddenly dropped from on high. That bell was magical.

"Older children take your places and please sit down. New children please stay here." Miss Marianne gave her friendliest smile as Dieter looked up from studying the knot in the floorboards between his sandals.

"I have a surprise for you." With that she reached under her desk and dragged out a large suitcase.

"Now let me see................Olga this is for you."

Dieter was amazed as Fraulein gave Olga a large decorated cardboard cone stuffed full of sweets and biscuits of every imaginable kind and then some. If he was extremely lucky he might get one or two sweets or a biscuit when he went shopping with Oma but only once in a while. He hoped Olga would share. Hang on a minute. There were more.

"Here you are Franz."

Dieter waited in line. It looked as though they were all getting a Zuckertuete. Wait till he showed Oma and Opa tonight. He could not possibly eat that many sweets in a day but he would certainly do his best. On it went. Dieter smiled at Helmut as they watched and waited. At last Fraulein flicked the suitcase shut with her foot and slid it back under her desk.

"That's all. Please go to your seats."

Dieter looked at Helmut and Helmut stared back. There was nothing for them. Tears threatened once more. Fraulein patted their heads as they stumbled to their desk. There Dieter stared at a spot that had been stained with ink. The edges were ragged where the ink had followed the grain before soaking into the wood. Gradually Dieter's eyes cleared and he looked dolefully at Helmut.

"When I get one I'll share it with you," he whispered. Helmut just nodded.

So school began. With such a large class Fraulein had her work cut out. She took no nonsense from the children and most of the time everything ran smoothly like a well-oiled machine. When the children came in each morning Miss Marianne had the day's lessons written up on the blackboard for each class. After the crisp "Good morning Children" and the drawn out "Good morning Fraulein ," she set each grade their work. Then she circulated, helping this one, prodding that one. At times some of the older children helped the young ones. Everything worked with German precision.

At playtime Dieter and Helmut followed the other children down the stairs, out into the sunshine and along the street to a farmhouse nearby. Everyone filed into the low cool basement where three village mothers stood behind a sturdy table. A large milk can stood on the floor. Two at a time the children walked up and held out their mugs. Dieter watched as one of the women used a long-handled dipper to pour milk into his cup. He was poised to take a sip when the girl behind nudged him and said, "Out of the way."

He moved away and followed the procession outside. As he drank his milk he peered over the top of the mug looking for Helmut. He couldn't see him anywhere. Helmut was not with the boys kicking a ball around, nor was he playing chase with the children who rushed past Dieter bumping his arm, causing him to spill some milk.

"Dieter." There he was behind him, sitting on a step. Dieter joined him and sat down to chat.

When the bell rang they filed back into the classroom, some chattering loudly to make up for lost time over the holidays.

"Now it's time to write numbers." Fraulein tapped the blackboard with her pointer. "Firstly let's count to ten." One by one the children stuttered and stumbled their way to ten. Dieter felt quite proud of himself. He may not have a Zuckertuete but he could count to ten no trouble. Next the teacher pointed to apples on the board, groups of apples in boxes. They took it in turns telling how many apples there were in each box. Then she wrote the number underneath.

"Your work is to copy the pictures and numbers onto your slates as neatly as you can. When you've finished put your hand up and I'll check it."

Dieter set to with gusto. He raised the lid on the desk and nearly sent Olga's Zuckertuete flying. She glared at him as she clutched it and they took out their slates. His concentration was intense as he leant over his desk and drew the first box. Next he put a fat juicy apple inside. Wow! It looked delicious. Carefully he drew **1** underneath. Problems started when he had to draw more and more apples in the boxes. He scrubbed at five apples with his fist. They refused to fit in the box. He glanced at Olga's slate. What a good idea. She was drawing the apples first and then making a box to fit. She rubbed out a crooked line with her duster. Dieter did the same. He wiped off the last box with apples sticking out the top and started again.

"Well done Dieter. That's good." Fraulein had crept up from behind, completely unnoticed.

It seemed no time at all before it was lunch time. They followed the same routine as before but this time they took their plates as well. Dieter breathed in the smell appreciatively as he entered the basement. He craned his neck from the back of the queue but was unable to see what smelled so good. Then a large girl with plaits walked past with her bowl – macaroni with milk and sugar. Mmmm! He licked his lips in anticipation. When his bowl and mug was full Dieter returned to the classroom taking care not to spill a drop as he climbed the stairs. He sat down at his desk and tucked in. Fraulein put an older girl in charge of the lunch time proceedings and slipped downstairs for her own lunch at home above the saddlery. Her mother would have it ready for her. Thank goodness not all the children stayed for lunch – only the refugee children and those from large families who had difficulty supporting them all from a small farm.

The afternoon session was shorter for the beginners. Fraulein sat at her desk and called children from the back of the room to stand up and read to the class. Some faltered and stumbled over the words but others read so well.

"Good work, Hannelore," Fraulein smiled and nodded.

Dieter knew he would be able to read like that one day and it wouldn't be long, Fraulein Marianne said so. Everyone at home was impressed with his reading too.

At last the new class was dismissed. Dieter took his leather school bag down from the hook and packed his slate and mug, plate and cutlery. Very carefully he stowed his new reader. He slung the bag on his back and walked out with Franzl and Monika. The three children walked at a leisurely pace. Monika skipped along beside her brother and when she spoke her words seemed to skip along too with bumps and lumps as her feet met the ground again. They walked in silence as they cut through the fields on a well worn track. Franzl led the way as he was a year older than the other two. They skirted the field where the men were harvesting barley and then parted to go to their homes. It did not seem to take long to cover the distance.

Dieter rushed in to tell Oma all about his first day at school.

"…and we had macaroni with milk and sugar for lunch."

"Well," said Oma.

"And here's my reader. Fraulein said I'll soon be able to read it from cover to cover."

Oma tousled his hair. "I'm sure she's right."

CHAPTER TWENTY-ONE

It was January 1948. Dieter had done well in school for the six months last year and now here he was in Grade Two. He had moved further back in the classroom towards the big boys that he admired and held in awe. The winter cold outside was kept at bay by the stove in the front of the room. A crisp burning smell of wood wafted around. Naked bulbs lit the room, shedding light on the children bent over their tasks. The scritch of styli on slates could be heard amongst the sniffling snuffles and shuffling. Dieter was learning the wonders of the abacus. Oma had bought it for him at the grocery store. The coloured beads clacked as he concentrated on his sums. Wait till he told Oma and Opa what he was doing in Grade Two. It wouldn't be long now till school finished for the day.

Fraulein sat at her desk and observed the class with satisfaction. Sometimes she wondered why she persisted in this job but she too had come with her family as refugees from Poland. They had lost so much during the war that family and security held her tightly in their grasp. Maybe one day she would marry and move away from her parents. But today was different. The children were working well and she felt like the lady of the manor watching her servants bowed over their work in her presence. A small voice broke her reverie.

"Please Fraulein?"

"Yes."

"May I go to the toilet?"

"No Dieter you may not!" A frown creased her brow.

Dieter continued with his sums. He couldn't understand it. Just ten minutes ago Karl had been allowed out to the toilet. Dieter wriggled on his bench trying to hang on. It was difficult to concentrate on sums when you are busting.

"Please Fraulein," he called more urgently.

"I said no, so don't ask again."

Dieter was getting frantic now. A big boy in Grade Two should not wet his pants! Eventually he could hang on no longer and he hung his head in shame as pee puddled on the floor. Snickers came from children around him.

"Excuse me Fraulein, Dieter's peed his pants."

"Well he can sit in it till school's over. Get on with your work."

When it was time to go home Dieter put on his coat and left the classroom as quickly as possible. He kept his eyes down so he could not see the smirks on the children's faces. He wondered what he had done wrong to be singled out like that. He stumbled home on his own, blinking vigorously to clear his vision from the threatening tears. At home he could hold them back no longer.

"What's the matter Dieterle?"

"I wet my pants and all the children laughed."

"That's not like you. What happened?"

"Well," he sobbed "I asked to go to the toilet and Miss Marianne said no."

"Were you naughty?"

"No, she'd just let Karl go not long before I asked."

"Well never mind. We'll get you some dry pants and I'm sure it won't happen again."

But it did happen again. Several times. The final straw came when Dieter pooed his pants in school. How the children guffawed – well not the ones sitting near him. They held their noses and made noises of disgust.

"Off you go home and get yourself clean." Miss Marianne shunted him out the door and closed it firmly behind him. She hoped there would not be any repercussions this time. All the way home Dieter wondered what he was doing wrong. Was Miss Marianne trying to punish him for something? He was as quiet and obedient as any of his other classmates. Yet he was the only one who was not allowed to go to the toilet during class.

At home Oma quizzed him again but got no more answers than any other time. She heaved a sigh as Liesl took him to the river and stripped him off to wash him in the cold water. She scrubbed his clothes too with her nose wrinkled in distaste. At the back of her mind was a little niggling thought but she brushed it aside as she finished her task. That evening when Dieter was in bed he heard the low murmurings as Oma and Opa discussed the day.

"I want to know what is going on. I will visit school tomorrow on my way home."

Opa going to school! At last Dieter might find out what he had done wrong. He went to sleep with little comfort from the thought.

After school the next day Opa detoured through the streets of Muersbach. The lights were still burning in the school house he noted with satisfaction as he walked down the cobbled street and into the school building. At the top of the stairs he knocked loudly at the door.

"Yes." Fraulein Marianne opened the door. "Why, Herr Klier, come in."

Opa noted she looked harried as she motioned to a chair by her desk. "How may I help you?"

"It's about Dieter soiling himself in school yesterday. He says you will not allow him to go to the toilet. Is that right?"

"He should go at lunch time."

"But you allow other children to go to the toilet after lunch."

"That's not the point. Dieter needs to learn."

Opa thumped the desk making the blackboard duster and Fraulein Marianne jump.

"It never happens at home. It will not happen at school." With that he strode from the room, down the stairs and home.

It did not happen again. From then on Dieter was allowed to go to the toilet when he asked and Liesl breathed a sigh of relief.

There was much to learn and school life improved after that. However Fraulein seemed to ignore him. He was no longer asked to read in class. Dieter had a good memory so he listened and watched what went on around him. It appeared that was not enough. At the end of his first year at school in June Dieter's report card announced that he had failed miserably. Fives in all subjects!

"There is something odd here." Opa and Oma knew that Dieter's reading had improved dramatically to the point where he read anything he could get his hands on. Even the street signs with their big long names. Yet the report card said – Reading 5.

In July when school went back Dieter stayed in Grade Two.

"Mind you," said Oma, "he's completed Grade One in six months."

Still Opa was not convinced. Something fishy was going on.

"How was school today?" Opa asked him.

"All right," Dieter replied in a small voice. He had lost much of his exuberance for learning. Opa quizzed Heinz and Rudi but their only comment was "Ask Liesl." Of course Liesl knew 'nothing,' she replied in a bright and breezy way as she took off on one of her visits to friends.

"There is nothing for it. I want to get to the bottom of this. I will go back to school."

True to his word Opa turned up in front of Fraulein's desk once the children had gone home the next day. Her face blanched as she greeted her visitor.

"Fraulein Marianne, it seems that everything is not going well for Dieter at school."

"He is very young for Grade Two, Herr Klier."

"But what we see at home does not add up with his report card. He is a bright boy but he has lost his enthusiasm for school. What is going on?"

"I …. I do not know."

"Does it have anything to do with my daughter Liesl?"

Fraulein straightened the books on her desk and stood to her feet. A sob escaped her lips as she fled from the classroom. Opa heard her hurried steps echo down the stairs. Slowly he nodded to himself as he followed in a more dignified manner. The sun shone down on him as the light dawned in his mind. His hunch was correct but what had Liesl been doing? As he strode home he developed a plan of action. First he would need some concrete evidence before he confronted Liesl. She was adept at telling people only what she wanted them to know, what was in her best interests. Heinz would be the one to ask.

Dieter was outside playing with Luchs when Opa arrived.

"Watch, Opa!" Dieter threw a stick and Luchs tore off to fetch it, bringing it back to Dieter's feet.

"He's a clever dog. Did you teach him that?"

"Yes."

Opa went inside. Heinz had just brought some wood in and was washing up ready for dinner.

"Tell me, is Liesl part of the problem with Fraulein Marianne?"

"Well she could be," Heinz answered slowly.

"Why?"

"Well at the dances Liesl often moves in to dance with her man."

"Who is he?"

"Not just one. Whoever she is dancing with that night."

"How long has this been going on?"

"Oh, most of this year I'd say."

"But why does Liesl do this?"

"I think it's just a game with her. She doesn't seem to like any one in particular."

"The little minx. I'll put a stop to this." While Dieter was still outside Opa talked to Liesl alone.

"What is this I hear about you at the dances?" Opa asked.

Liesl stared fixedly at her hands.

"You are moving in on all of Fraulein Marianne's admirers."

"Maybe," Liesl mumbled.

"You are young to be going to the dances. Perhaps you should stay home till you grow up a bit more."

She looked sulkily at her father. Was he serious?

"Enough is enough!" Opa raised his voice and fixed her with a steely gaze. "Why should Dieter be punished and held back at school because of your behavior?" He shook his finger in her face. "Any more of it and I will spank you. Do you understand?"

"Yes Papa." Liesl picked at the quick around her thumb nail. She knew that the cat was out of the bag and she could not deny it.

CHAPTER TWENTY-TWO

Dieter was still in Grade Two. It was not so bad now Fraulein Marianne was kind to him again. The sun shone and the birds sang as the children played games in the street at lunchtime. After lunch when the bell rang the children lined up two by two outside. This afternoon they were going to the High School where grades five to eight went. Today they would be learning Social Studies. The long tail of children followed the teacher through the cobbled streets, past women chatting together with their baskets of produce resting at their feet. Small children played nearby. The school children talked together, some laughing, a happy bunch, as they wound up to the big school beside the church, opposite the priest's house.

At the top of the stairs Herr Hilgersmann met them. "Good afternoon." He nodded politely to Fraulein Marianne. He was a gentle, unassuming man with grey hair and spectacles. He wore a long-sleeved shirt with a button to the neck sleeveless pullover on top. Dieter liked the antler buttons on it. It reminded him of Opa Doerre who had buttons like that. Herr Hilgersmann ushered the children in with a smile.

"Take your seats in the front. That's right. Quickly now!"

It was dim inside. Most of the windows were darkened with only two letting sunlight into the room. A screen at the front hung over the blackboard.

"Move along. There's room for one more."

Finally everyone was packed in and a tall boy with sticking out ears used a hook on the end of a pole to lower the other blackouts into place. The coughing and shuffling stopped as a beam of light lit up the screen and a countdown flickered past. Dieter thought it was amazing. He had never seen a film before. The newsreel showed different trades in Germany. Although there was no sound or commentary he could almost hear and feel the huge locomotive being driven across the screen by the engine driver. There were charcoal makers in the forest and carpenters building houses. The part that left the greatest impression was the ceramics factory. Dieter sat mesmerized as he watched strong hands mould the clay on the wheel to make a bowl, a plate and a tall jug. All he saw were the hands and the clay in close up, nothing else. They seemed to be working in unison as the clay responded to the man's strong hands.

When the lights came on and the blackouts were taken down Dieter blinked as he came back to the present. It was time to go home from school and he could not wait to tell Oma and Opa about the film.

"A wonderment, just a wonderment."

Oma smiled at him and Opa nodded.

"How can they put moving pictures like that on a screen. The man wasn't even there but I saw him make pots."

"Yes Dieter. It's very clever isn't it?"

"The man was clever too. His hands just moved like this and he made a beautiful bowl."

"You really enjoyed that."

"Yes I want to do that one day."

"Maybe you will. Now get your hands washed for dinner."

Dieter was a diligent student bent over his slate, tongue out the corner of his mouth as he concentrated on his writing. Today he was practicing walking sticks, some up the right way and some upside down. Rows of them, first this way, then that. He had not realised that there were so many walking sticks to help letters walk through the alphabet. Oh well, he was getting better at writing them.

"Put your slates away now children. I'll look at your writing later." Fraulein had been checking mathematics with the older pupils. "His Reverence will be here any minute."

The priest was a tall heavily built man. He came to the school regularly in his long black cassock and biretta, a three-cornered hat with a pom-pom on top. His Reverence seemed to fill the doorway as he came in. The class clattered to their feet as they bowed.

"Praise be Jesus Christ," they chanted in unison.

"In all eternity," the priest replied.

"Amen." The children sat down again as he picked up the cane from the blackboard groove.

"Now the Catechism. Who remembers it?" He pointed the cane at a girl three rows behind Dieter. If only he chose a second child before Dieter all would be well. He did not want to feel the cane on his fingers or backside any more. As soon as one or two children had recited the Catechism he would remember it again too. Dieter much preferred the Old Testament stories but they came after this ordeal was over. Straining to listen, Dieter knew there was no time for daydreaming now. Once he had heard Opa call His Reverence the "black devil" and he knew why.

CHAPTER TWENTY-THREE

It was the summer holidays. Oma put her broom back in the corner.
"Dieter, where are you?"
Dieter came scurrying in.
"We're off to Hoefen now." Dieter liked going to Hoefen. A
toymaker from Bohemia lived there. Maybe he would get a new toy
today. He knew the routine he must go through before they left. Go
to the lavatory, wash your face and hands. Oma straightened his hair
as she tilted his face up towards her.
"You'll do!" She planted a kiss on his cheek. The sun shone down on
them as they left Zaugendorf and walked along the lanes through
pasture and fields of potatoes, tall golden barley and sugar beet. Oma
carried a large basket over her arm. Dieter darted here and there,
walking twice as far as Oma she was sure. He crouched down on his
haunches looking into the stalks of barley as they waved in the
breeze, fascinated by the changing patterns of shade and light. Just as
Oma caught up he was off again as something else caught his eye.
Oma hummed to herself. It was a pleasant time of day to be out for a
walk.

As they came to Freudeneck Dieter hung back and held onto
Oma's hand. Here they often stopped at the Village Inn.
"Are you thirsty after all your ducking and diving?" Oma asked.
Dieter nodded.
"I am too," Oma added. So in they went. She rummaged in her
basket and pulled out a pair of socks with the toes neatly sewn up
again.
"Lemonade and a bread roll please."
The innkeeper smiled. He needed new socks and he knew not to ask
questions. He slipped them under the counter.
"Certainly," he said as he bustled around.
Oma took the tall glass of lemonade and the roll to the table.

"Lovely day out there."

"Yes it is. We're on our way to Hoefen."

"Mr Toyman lives there," said Dieter.

Oma smiled as she passed the glass to Dieter.

"Drink up, but leave some for me." She broke the bread roll in half as Dieter's eyes watched her over the top of the glass. He licked his lips as he put the glass down and took the plate from Oma. She sipped the lemonade appreciatively. A quick wipe of face and hands and they were on their way once more.

Dieter could hear the bees buzzing about their business. The birds chirped a chorus as he skipped along by Oma's side. He did not visit Hoefen very often now that he was at school. The first house they came to in the village belonged to Mr Toyman. Well, he lived at one end of the top storey and his workshop ran the length of the remaining floor space. Sunshine streamed in the windows casting squares of light on his bench and spilled onto the floor. He whistled as he sanded a toy boat.

"Hello there!" He looked up and smiled as the bell jangled when they opened the door.

"What are you after today?"

"We'll have a look first if you don't mind." Oma did not want to spend too much. Certainly, she was bartering with articles of clothing her men acquired from the American Army Base where they worked but they still had to be careful. She used the goods to barter for food as well when she could. Otherwise they would never make it into their own home. Dieter dragged Oma round the workshop. He liked the pecking hens, but no, this looked better.

"Bricks Oma. Look at this." He pointed to a box of building blocks that looked like miniature bricks. "I'd be able to build a whole village with that."

"It's too pricey Dieterle, another time maybe."

He liked the dancing lady but he already had one of those hanging on the wall. There was a clown on a string to swing around. It was a hard decision.

"What about one of these?" The toymaker placed a little man on a sloping board and he waddled down on his own.

"Let me try." Dieter placed him at the top of the board and increased the slope. The little man ran as fast as he could and fell in a heap at the bottom. Dieter laughed. "Yes, I like him."

"All right," said Oma. She gave him to Dieter as she drew a thick shirt from her basket. Dieter turned the man over in his hands looking at the bright colours of his clothes. Mr Toyman examined the shirt. Oma pointed to the building blocks and raised her eyebrows in a questioning manner.

"Enough?" she asked.

In reply Mr Toyman handed her the bricks and helped her to conceal them in the basket under her cardigan.

"Thank you." There were smiles all round as they parted. Mr Toyman was happy with his new shirt, Oma was happy with the Christmas surprise and Dieter was very happy with his new toy.

"Now let's see how the Hajeks are going." Oma headed down the street. The Hajeks had come from Bohemia too. In fact there was quite a settlement of people from Czechoslovakia in this area who had fled for their lives and lost everything. Mr and Mrs Hajek lived not far from the toymaker's place and soon there were cries of welcome and delight when they arrived.

"How are you?" Mrs Hajek hugged Oma then turned her attention to Dieter. "My, haven't you grown. I hear you're a big school boy now." Being a bit deaf, she was inclined to shout as though Dieter was deaf too.

"See what I've got!" He held up the little man for her to admire.

"Well aren't you lucky. Why don't you find Mr Hajek out in the yard and talk to him while I make Oma some coffee. Have you had lunch?" She turned to Elli.

"We've had something to eat at Freudeneck," Oma added hastily.

"But you'll still need coffee!"

"Yes that would be welcome."

She bustled around as Oma sat at the table and watched. There was no doubt her dear friend from home was getting older and not able to move so quickly now.

"How are you?"

"I'm well enough. Sometimes my knees ache. I want to be able to look after little Johanna while Maria works. If I can do that I will be happy."

"Yes," Oma nodded thinking similar thoughts. She was younger than her friend but sometimes she felt very tired too.

Mr Hajek and Dieter came in as Oma helped Mrs Hajek pour coffee into the cups and place them on the table. She put out some small coffee rolls.

"In case the young man is hungry."

Dieter proved her right as he took the proffered roll and glass of milk.

"And how are Maria and the child?"

"They are well. Maria works so hard to make life better for us. I wish I could help more so that she could rest a little."

"Yes but that's what she wants to do. She remembers life in Bruex and what you left behind. We are the lucky ones who made it out. We still have each other."

"I know. When you think of Soukob our life is good."

"We were talking about our old friend Soukob just the other day," Mr Hajek interjected. "His furniture was of such high quality that I had no trouble selling it. Often I had people ordering it before it left the factory."

"Yes he was a good man. He lost so much. It is better that he passed on to his rest."

There was a lull in the conversation as each one remembered Soukob and what they had lost when they left Bruex.

"Everything's different now," Mrs Hajek added.

"Yes I'm thankful for a new start. Josef and the boys are working so hard. Soon we'll have our own home. We must make a fresh start for the sake of the little ones."

CHAPTER TWENTY-FOUR

Sun streamed through the window as Erika woke up. Today was her brother's wedding. Christa was still sleeping. Usually she was awake by now. Erika sat up in bed and prodded Werner.

"Please light the stove."

"In a minute," he said as he rolled over.

Erika humphed in annoyance as she got out of bed and straightened her white tricot petticoat that doubled as a nightgown. Her dusky pink dress hung on the rail. Erika was pleased with the way it had turned out. It had a v-neck and four buttons down the front just past the waist. The sleeves were slightly gathered at the shoulders but slim lined. As she put on her dress she admired the way the flaired skirt hung over her slim hips. She still had a good figure even after giving birth to two children. She pointed her toes as she sat on a stool and slipped her feet into her stockings, adjusting the seams carefully. It was a shame that she was unable to find better shoes but her brown lace-ups would have to do. After brushing her dark wavy hair she leant closer to the mirror to examine her eyebrows. She took a used match and rubbed it over her eyebrows to darken them. It was amazing what you had to do to maintain your good looks at the end of a war!

Over at Dirauf's Opa was stoking the fire with small twigs and coaxing the stove into life. Oma threw back the blankets and stretched, then put her feet to the floor. Their oldest son was getting married today! No time for lying in bed. There was so much to do. It was a cool morning but it promised to be a fine day. She chose her best dress from the wardrobe and pulled it on, doing up the buttons down the front. The colour suited her, navy with white flowers. Oma straightened the roll collar and arranged the ties loosely to hang down the front. She had made it herself some time ago out of a soft cotton material. It wasn't new but she felt good in it as she smoothed it down over her body. Sitting on the bed she pulled on her stockings and slipped into her old house-shoes. Her white lace-ups would wait until it was time to go. As she brushed her hair she glanced at Dieter sleeping peacefully in his bed. He had been so excited last evening. She hoped that he would sleep longer while she prepared breakfast. She wound her long dark hair into a bun and pinned it in place. Next she donned her striped apron to keep her dress clean. Heinz and Gerti's wedding. What a celebration it will be! No one had known about Erika and Werner getting married till well after their wedding when they moved to a nearby village.. Today would be special.

Dieter skipped along holding Opa's hand. Oma carried a basket with Dieter's wedding clothes laid across it on top of his new white shoes. It would be asking for trouble to dress him in white for the walk to Muersbach where Mr and Mrs Rudolf, the bride's parents lived. They had fled Silesia during the war and also lived in two rooms in a farmhouse in Muersbach. They were kindly, gentle folk and had arranged for the celebration to take place at the farmhouse after the wedding ceremony.

"Tell me what you have to do at the wedding," said Opa. "I've forgotten."

"Oh Opa! I haven't forgotten."

"Good, as long as you remember everything."

"Here we are," said Oma.

It took a while for their eyes to adjust from the bright sunlight as they entered the Rudolf home. The singing of birds gave way to chattering and laughter. Large pots of soup were bubbling on the stove and the smell of chickens and ducks roasting mingled in the air.

At long last it was time for Dieter to get dressed for the wedding. Oma had begun preparations the day before. Dieter's hair was neatly trimmed and he had enjoyed a warm bath in the tub in front of the stove before bed. The bath had helped him to sleep because he was so excited. Now he could put on his sailor suit. He had tried it on so many times while Mari made it for him. But now it was complete. Dieter was the page boy at Heinz and Gerti's wedding. Oma helped him as he slid into his long trousers. He pulled the top over his head and Oma straightened the square collar edged with navy blue. She tied the ends to hang in front and stood back to admire him. Dieter struggled with his new white socks then slipped his feet into white canvas shoes. This was an important occasion. He did not remember ever having a complete new outfit before. In his mind he went over his instructions again.

"Walk behind Gerti, holding her train just so. If you walk too fast you will stand on her dress! If you walk too slowly you will pull her tiara off her head. Just watch Gerti and think what you are doing." He could do it. He knew he could. How many practices had they had? Lots! Last evening Gerti had given him a chocolate because he had done it so well.

"If I do it well today ….. do you think Gerti has any chocolates left?"

"You'll not be eating any in your white suit!" Oma emphasized.

"Everyone ready? Let's go!"

Heinz was keen to get to the church. He felt there was too much talk and not enough action. Gerti's sister made final adjustments to Gerti's veil and headgear.

"You look beautiful and the sun is smiling down on you." Heinz said. Gerti smiled and turned adoringly to Heinz as she took his arm. The procession wound around through the village and up to St Sebastian's Church. Dieter walked proudly behind Gerti holding the delicate veil between thumbs and first fingers as he had been shown. He did not look at the well wishers or even his school mates lining the streets but he knew they were there. He heard Helmut call his name but he was concentrating on his important task. If he did it very well……. who knew? The church spire with the orb and cross on top grew closer and closer, beckoning them. It was tricky going up the steps to the church courtyard but Dieter remembered Gerti's instructions – *"Just watch and think what you're doing."*

At last they were standing at the church door. Dieter peeped round past Gerti and saw Father Schugmann standing in front of the altar. The congregation was already seated and the organ was playing. The Klier and Rudolf parents walked up the aisle and took their seats. Now it was their turn. *"Just watch and think what you're doing."* Dieter felt his responsibility keenly as he followed the bride and groom up the aisle for the nuptial mass. Heinz and Gerti lowered themselves to the kneeler while Dieter dutifully held the train. As the priest intoned the mass Dieter breathed in the smell of incense and beeswax candles. It was a familiar smell that brought comfort to him. He thought back to the time when he had come into the church alone after playing with his mates. He knew it was God's house. Father Schugmann had told them at school and he wanted to be near

God. He was tired and laid down in front of the altar. He did not remember any more after that but Rudi had told him later. It was getting late and Rudi had been sent to look for him. Finally he tracked him down to the church and found him fast asleep. He picked him up gently and with Dieter's head resting on his shoulder Rudi had walked back to Zaugendorf with the little lost lamb..... Dieter came to with a start at a loud "AMEN" from Father Schugmann. *"Just watch and think what you're doing."* Well he didn't have to think too much just now or watch because he was standing still. His eyes wandered to the Marien Altar on the right side of the church. A white lace cloth edged the altar with an imposing red marble backdrop towering above it. An angel with golden wings perched on top where he could look down on the ceremony and also look out the window from time to time. Dieter could see only the blue cloudless sky and the sun shining through the window. He liked the way the rays kissed the potted pink hydrangeas on one side of the altar. The others were beautiful too but they were in the shade. A small shadow flitted across the flowers as a bird flew past the window. His eyes roamed to the golden framed baroque inset on the altar. It contained a soft vision of Mary holding Jesus in her arms. White marble pillars, entwined around with grape vines, spiraled up beside the mother and child.

"In the name of the Father, Son and Holy Ghost, Amen."

Dieter woke from his reverie as Father Schugmann pronounced the blessing on the newlyweds. Now he needed to watch and think again.

Heinz and Gerti stood up and Dieter stepped to one side as they turned, then walked down the aisle. Children with baskets strewed petals in front of them as the bridal party walked down the church steps and across the courtyard. The bells rang out to let the whole village know the happy news. There were many more well-wishers now as they retraced their journey back to the Rudolf's home. Everyone smiled and waved, calling out greetings to the young couple. Dieter felt very tired when at last they walked back into the farmhouse living room. It was all the excitement and the concentration. Then of course he had to stand still holding the train for the entire wedding service in the church. At last he could relax.

The banquet tables, covered in white damask cloths, were set out in a u-shape round the outside of the room. Heinz held the chair for Gerti as she sat down and helped Dieter arrange her train. At last he could let go. How his arms and fingers ached! Oma kissed her new daughter in law on the cheek.

"Welcome to our family. Now we have a second Mrs Klier." Gerti smiled. Oma took Dieter by the hand.

"Come Dieterle. There is a special seat for my boy. I am very proud of you. What a splendid job. Now it is time to eat."

Once everyone was seated ladies in white aprons carried in steaming soup tureens. Dieter's eyes opened wide as Oma lifted the lid. Noodle soup and so much of it. She took his bowl and ladled in a generous helping.

"Be careful, it's hot." She blew on it a little before setting the bowl in front of him. Dieter put some on his spoon and blew gently. He watched little waves rippling across the soup in front of his nose. He sipped it gingerly. Ah!! The smell was good and it looked delicious but the taste was even better. Slowly, methodically, a spoonful, blow gently, sip and Dieter finished the bowl.

"Excuse me please." Opa moved aside to let a waitress put a platter on the table – roast chicken and dumplings floating in gravy. More food came, duck swimming in sauce with dumplings that looked like ducklings fanning out in its wake, bowls of cauliflower in white sauce and cabbage.

"What would you like now? Some duck?"

Dieter's eyes turned to the tureen.

"More soup please." He could not go past the soup, eating bowl after bowl. Oma and Opa watched on in amusement.

"Let him be," said Opa. "It's good nourishing soup and he's enjoying himself."

"Yes, he needs fattening up. He's so thin." Oma worried about him but it seemed there was not much she could do about it. Oh well, today was a day of celebration. The food was wonderful. The farmer where the Rudolf's lived had certainly been generous. He was more kindly disposed towards them than Dirauf had been. But she mustn't complain. Soon they would move into their own home.

Still more food came. Fruit compote, creamy custard, tortes. They had not seen so much food since leaving Bruex. Finally Dieter had opted for something other than noodle soup. A plate with a wedge of torte sat in front of him. The layers of jam and butter cream looked enticing. He made feeble attempts with a spoon, picking bits from here and there. The truth of the matter was, he was full up to pussy's ribbon. Waitresses were still bustling around serving coffee, wine and beer to the tables. Dieter gave up and just sat and watched. He was satisfied with his choice and to think he had as much as he wanted.

The host farmer came out with his piano accordion and sat at the far end of the room. The syncopated rhythm of the folk music set feet tapping. Strauss waltzes beckoned people to dance. Dieter settled against Rudi and watched contentedly. Couples danced then sat down to drink schnapps or whatever they fancied while others took their place on the dance floor. Heinz and Gerti floated past in a beautiful waltz with eyes only for each other. Dieter was feeling decidedly sleepy when Gerti came back and tapped him on the shoulder.

"For a special boy. Thank you!" She gave him a cellophane bag of chocolates. Each one was individually wrapped in silver foil with a picture on it – an umbrella chocolate, a hammer, a rabbit. Dieter was awake by now.

"All for me?"

"Yes Dieter but not all at once or you'll be sick. Have you got a pocket?"

"No."

"Well ask Oma to look after this for you." She took his hand and pressed two shiny coins into it. Goodness. His very own money to spend. Dieter went over to Oma.

"Look after this please till I go to the shop."

"What will you buy?" Oma asked.

"I'll have a look first."

Oma smiled as he snuggled up to her. Dieter felt that it had been the best day of his life. Firstly he had needed brand new clothes for the occasion. Then he had more food than he could believe and now chocolates and his own money to spend as he pleased. People smiled at him and patted his head, telling him he had done a fine job. Yes, it had been well worth it he thought as he drifted off to sleep leaning against Oma.

CHAPTER TWENTY-FIVE

No school today because it was Saturday. Dieter had enjoyed playing outside in the sunshine. It was late Spring and he played on the hill just behind the farmhouse, his favourite spot in the pine forest. Green moss covered the rocks and Dieter spent many happy hours there making paths for the little people, always hoping to see them. He was good at spotting where they had been but had never seen them out and about yet. They made their homes in the nooks and crannies between rocks and round the base of the cracked tree trunks.

Today he had found a soft feather and some dandelion seed heads that felt like down. Carefully he gathered the softness in his hands and made a hollow for it in the moss. Next he put twigs around the outside. He guessed they would use it for their tiny people and he was afraid they might fall out. The problem was he did not know how big or small to make it. Oh well, they could put more than one baby in it if it was too big. It was so soft. He laid his little finger in it and it felt wonderful.

Gradually Dieter worked his way through the forest, looking, digging, poking – carefully. He did not want to disturb the little people if they were sleeping. On the other side he came out into the sunshine and wound down through the silver birches to a hollow. Here there were many rocks covered by a carpet of moss. It looked like a landscape of rolling green hills. Dieter lay on his stomach and watched the beetles scurrying helter-skelter this way and that. He wondered where they were going and where they had been. One was trying to drag something. Dieter moved closer to see what it was but the beetle hurried away through the moss. Maybe she had been to market and was taking food home to the family. Surely a basket would have made it easier but he supposed she needed all her legs for clambering up and over the hills.

By now Dieter's stomach was rumbling so he meandered home to Oma.

"I thought you'd be home when you were hungry." Oma smiled. He was a good boy most of the time. But lately she was worried about his cough and thin little body. She must take him to the doctor. After lunch he played inside with his bricks, building this, building that, never short of ideas. He was a dreamer, always able to amuse himself. Well, he had to with no younger siblings around, only adults. Although Erika had moved closer to them she never bothered to keep in touch. Dieter probably would not recognise her if he saw her.

As the day wore on the sun moved across the sky and it was becoming cooler. Oma was at the stove preparing the evening meal. She jumped and dropped her ladle into the pot as she heard Dirauf shouting.

"Get out! We don't want you here."

My, he was an angry man. Who was he yelling at now? Oma fished her ladle out of the stew and wiped her hands on the dish cloth. She looked out the window. A cry of alarm escaped her lips as she saw him raise a stick to Erika. Oma ran out the door with Dieter in hot pursuit. He must be mad.

"Go away. I know all about you." Whack! He brought the stick down sharply on her back. Erika was lying in the shadows on the ramp to the front door.

"We don't want you and your bastards here! Go back where you came from."

Whack! As Erika drew her knees up around her pregnant belly and cradled her head in her arms, Dieter looked on in horror. Oma and Frau Dirauf were crying.

"Stop it you brute," Oma called out.

"We've got enough hangers on stuffed into our house."

Whump! Dieter could take no more. Oma was his life, the one who had cared for him all his life, but something sparked within him for this other woman.

"Mutti! Mutti!" He threw himself over his mother, sobbing uncontrollably. Dirauf could not continue. He lowered his weapon and marched around the corner of the house muttering "bloody refugees." Oma and Frau Dirauf helped Erika to her feet.

"Are you all right?" Oma asked. Erika nodded, her eyes brimming with tears.

94

"I don't know what's wrong with him. You expecting a baby and all." Frau Dirauf shook her head in disbelief. "I'll make you a cup of coffee."

Oma helped her daughter inside. She was shaken and had a welt darkening on her arm. Oma hoped the baby was unharmed. She lay Erika on the bed and covered her with a blanket. There was a knock on the door. Oma straightened her apron and pulled herself up to her full height as she opened the door. Dirauf had done enough damage. He was not coming in here. Wait till Josef hears about this. But it was Frau Dirauf with a basket and a steaming coffee pot.

"She's lying down," Oma said as she relaxed her mouth a little and peered down the passage.

"Take this. I am so sorry. I don't know what got into him."

"Thank you. Erika is all right I think. Time will tell whether all is well with the baby. Our own house will be ready soon and then you can have your house back. Thank you Mari. You are a kind soul." Oma took her hand and pressed it.

Frau Dirauf scuttled away as Oma closed the door. Dieter lay on the bed next to his mother stroking her hand.

"It's all right now Mutti. He's a bad man. I won't let him hit you again.

CHAPTER TWENTY-SIX

It was the summer of 1950. At last they were moving house. But this time they had planned the move to suit themselves. They were not fleeing as they had done from Bruex. Living with Diraufs had been better than wandering and sleeping wherever they could find a place but at times it had been unpleasant because of Herr Dirauf's attitude. Oma had feared for Erika and her unborn child after the beating he had meted out to her. She had no idea why his temper had suddenly erupted. Dirauf for his part had been pleased to hear that Herr Klier and sons were building their own house. At last they were moving and he would be rid of them. He was noticeable by his absence as the family loaded the last of their possessions onto the hand-pulled wagon. Opa settled the remnants of the kitchen goods into nooks and crannies among the bigger items. He took the feather blankets from Rudi and tucked them over the top and down the sides. Oma took a final look around the room checking to see that it was spick and span. Yes, everything was clean and tidy. As she shut the door for the last time she smiled to herself. My Peppi, you did it!

Maria hurried out to say goodbye. She pressed a warm loaf of bread into Oma's hands. "Here you'll need something for lunch while you get organized."

"Thank you my dear. You've been so kind to us."

"It is nothing. I thank God that we were not landed in your situation."

The sun shone down and warmed their backs as they set off along the road. Magpies were arguing in the trees by the river as they crossed the bridge. The metal bands around the wagon wheels crunched along the road. Opa's heart was light as he pulled the cart. Dieter walked alongside watching the sunlight dance through the spokes on the wheels, casting flickering shadows as they moved forward. Rudi put his shoulder to the wagon from behind, helping his father with the load.

Their own house! There it was standing proud. A little cottage made from ammunition packing cases supplied by the US Army depot where the men had been working. Oddments of timber lay scattered on the grass. There would be plenty of time to organize the yard later. After Dirauf's brutal attack Opa could not wait to turn his back on him.

"Come," he said as he led Oma to the door. With his arm on her shoulder he turned the handle and pushed the door open.

"Welcome to the Klier Hof."

With tears in her eyes and a song in her heart Oma looked around. A fine three roomed home! Peppi and her two strong sons had put their backs into building their home every weekend and in the evenings in the summer months as they put the final touches to the interior. After Heinz was married he had not been able to help as often but the basic structure was finished by then.

It was as though they had closed the gate on their homelessness and wandering when they left Diraufs. Now they were opening the door on their new life full of hopes and dreams. Opa and Rudi set to, unloading the wagon while Oma showed them where they should put things.

"Liesl your job is to make the beds and I'll put the kitchen to rights."

"Yes Mama."

Dieter wandered outside so that he would not get in the way. Behind the house was a grove of trees, tall oak trees. Dieter skipped around picking wildflowers as he went. White plumes of astilbe, bluebells, cornflowers and scarlet poppies at the edge of the meadow nearby.

"Look Oma," he announced when his little hands could not hold any more, "flowers for the table."

"Thank you, sweetheart." She took a jug from the bench and poured some water from the bucket into it. "These will look just beautiful in our new home."

Liesl busied herself making the beds. First she went through to her parents' room. She ran her hand over the smooth curves on the polished walnut wardrobe. Magnificent. The bed and side tables completed the suite. She tucked the sheet under the striped mattress stuffed with straw. This would be renewed each year. The feather quilt had been made by her mother. A red cotton fabric to hold the feathers and a floral print cover buttoned over it with pillow cases to match. Many evenings Liesl had watched her mother sitting by the stove at the farm deftly plucking the down from the feathers she had gathered that day. Bird life was plentiful along the river where they lived and in spring there was always an abundant supply of feathers. Mari had added to the bag of feathers every time she plucked a duck or goose. So with constant enterprise and effort she had made quilts and pillows for the whole family. Liesl plumped up the pillows and set them in place. She glanced around the room. White-wash on the wide boards that lined the room. They had used wooden rollers carved with a leaf pattern and rolled in a tray of paint to trail green foliage down the walls at regular intervals. The room looked fresh and beautiful. A breeze rippled through the open window.

Next she went through to her room adjacent to her parents' and made up the two camp stretchers. Dieter would sleep here too so that he would not be disturbed early in the morning when Opa and Rudi ate their breakfast and left for work in Bamberg. Liesl had chosen a flower pattern to grace her walls. Once the beds were made it looked wonderful. She had chosen well. She leant on the window sill gazing out at Opa and Rudi picking up wood in the yard. Aha! Maybe Mama wanted the combustion stove lit. She certainly felt like some lunch and a hot drink.

"Fetch me some more water from the well Liesl please."

"I'll help," chirped Dieter. It was such a novelty to get water from the well instead of the river. Oma cut thick slices of fresh bread and buttered them as she hummed to herself. She put the bread board on the table and set out cups from the shelf. More wood on the stove. So far she was impressed with her new combustion stove that Opa and the boys had installed. Tomorrow maybe she would make a cake and invite Heinz and Gerti to join them for afternoon coffee.

"Time to wash up," she called to the men. "Lunch is ready."

Opa and Rudi had been stacking the wood that was lying round the yard. They clumped up the steps and took their shoes off in the covered verandah. Opa admired the wooden washing machine he had managed to buy. It had a handle on the side to agitate the washing, making it much quicker and easier than washing by hand.

"Well here we are then." Opa sat on a chair and waited for the kettle to boil. He was ready for a coffee and something to eat. His eyes scanned their handiwork. The timber for the frames he had bought from the saw-mill and carted home in the wagon with the help of Heinz and Rudi. The outside walls were clad with packing cases from the army base. Several truck loads had been dropped off by the army. The inside was lined with thick boards made from wood wool glued and compressed. They would need the insulation in the winter. Thick tar paper tied down with battens covered the roof. Opa smiled to himself as he recalled the day he procured the recycled external doors and the windows. The Americans seemed to throw good things away and start again with new. He was pleased when they said he could have them for nothing. It had been a huge project but little by little they had completed it. Now he wanted to plant flowers around their home. In the meantime Dieter's wildflowers would do very nicely. Pink roses twined down the walls in the living area, from the frieze near the ceiling. It softened the stark white of the walls.

"Coffee, my dear." Oma placed his cup in front of him and the others drew their chairs up.

"It's beautiful Opa. I like our home."

"Thank you."

"And I do too." Oma passed the plate around and the family ate in silence, relishing the long awaited moment. Memories of Bruex and the family scattered around Germany was foremost in some minds. A number of them were only that now - alive in their memories. But here they were safe and well in their own humble abode.

"Anyone at home?" Heinz bounded up the steps and opened the door. "Well this looks cozy, so much better with you all living in it." Oma smiled.

"What's that you've got?" Dieter pointed to something large wrapped in a sheet under Heinz's arm.

He laid it down on Rudi's bed. Carefully he unwrapped it and held it up for everyone to see.

"Heinz, where did you get that?" Oma could not believe her eyes. It was a painting of the Schlossberg and Opa Doerre's garden next to it in Bruex.

"I painted it for you. It's to go above your bed."

"Oh thank you. How beautiful!" Oma took Heinz's face in both of her warm hands and planted a kiss first on one cheek, then the other. "So thoughtful and you did it yourself."

Opa led the way into the bedroom and held the picture up to the wall.

"Yes, it's perfect there. Get my hammer and nails please Rudi." In no time at all, the picture took pride of place above Oma and Opa's bed. "It's as though there is another window in our bedroom and I can look out on Schlossberg once more," Oma said as she wiped away tears with her apron. "I am at home. Thank you."

CHAPTER TWENTY-SEVEN

As the children left the classroom at the end of the day Fraulein called Dieter over. She held an envelope in her hand. "Herr und Frau Klier" was written in bold dark script across it.

"This is an important letter for your grandparents. Take it home. Do not lose it on the way!"

"Yes Fraulein." Dieter went to stuff it in his pocket.

"No not there. Put it in your bag and go straight home."

"Yes Fraulein." Dieter opened his bag and slipped it down the side. Then he shouldered his bag and walked down the stairs. Who was it from? It was not Fraulein's writing. Hers was small and neat. As he popped out into the sunshine he pulled his jacket around him. Although the spring thaw had finished it was still nippy in the mornings and later in the afternoon.

The other children had vanished so he would have to walk home alone. But what was in the letter? He walked along with his hands in his pockets, kicking a stone as he left Muersbach and walked on the path through the fields. Eventually he lost interest in the stone and wandered on deep in thought. Fraulein had said, 'Go straight home!' but he was awfully thirsty. Maybe he should go by Kathi's house and have a drink of the spring water in her basement. She lived more or less in the direction of 'straight home' and he could show the letter to Kathi. It must be important and it would be a shame not to show someone. It would not take long. He knocked on Kathi's door.

"Why hello Dieter. Have you seen my boys?"

"No I walked alone today."

"Why was that? Is everything all right?"

"Oh yes thank you. Fraulein kept me behind. She gave me an important letter for Oma and Opa." He rummaged in his bag and drew out the letter.

"See!" he held it up proudly.

"Well you need to run along and take it home. Are you thirsty today?" Kathi knew the routine.

"Yes I am. Could I have a drink of water please?"

"Here." She handed him a mug. "You know where it is. "I'll get you some bread too, if you like."

"Oh thank you. That would be lovely."

Kathi watched him as he scuttled off to the cellar. He was very thin and still coughed often. Thank goodness he looked better since his grandmother took him to the doctor but he was malnourished. Dieter came back with the clear spring water.

"Now you sit at the table while you eat your bread."

"Mmmm! Thank you." He took his first bite. It was fresh baked sour dough rye bread with a thick slather of butter. Dieter's favourite. Kathi watched him as he tucked in. It was four years now since the Klier family had arrived in Zaugendorf. She knew where they had come from but could only imagine what they had been through. Kathi looked around her kitchen. She was fortunate. This house had been in the family for centuries. It was old and still standing firm. They had felt the effects of the war with shortages and so forth but nothing like this family and others.

"That was delicious thank you." Dieter finished his water and wiped his mouth with the back of his hand.

"Now you'd better run along and take that letter home."

"I will. See you again."

"Yes, see you again." Kathi smiled as she watched him run off."

"Oma! Oma! I've got a letter for you." Dieter called as he burst into the room. Oma was washing vegetables in a bucket. Fresh vegetables from their own garden just down the road that Opa had planted before they moved in. The fire in the stove glowed, greeting him with warmth in contrast to the cool damp settling down outside. Dieter fished in his bag and flourished the letter.

"Here it is. For you and Opa. Fraulein gave it to me."

"Thank you. Now how about you go and get me some firewood while I sit down and read it. That's a good boy."

Oma pulled out a chair and sank onto it as she opened the letter. From the Director of Health. Dear God! She held it under the light as she read on ......

'It has come to our notice that your grandson Dieter Klier is suffering the after effects of tuberculosis and malnutrition. Therefore

we would like to offer him a placement in the Kinderheim at Fuessen for a period of eight weeks. You are required to go to the office in Ebern at the above address to make the necessary arrangements....'
She would miss the little scamp! She had done her best but he was still very thin. However, she'd heard about the Kinderheim and it had a very good reputation. On Friday they must go to Ebern.

Dieter chattered excitedly as they crunched along the path to Ebern. They had left early so that there would be time for lunch at Oma's favourite Gasthof. As they passed through Muersbach Dieter smiled as he looked up at the schoolroom windows. No school for him today, no Pfarrer Schugmann either. He skipped happily on.
"Oma, why do I have to see Doktor Stark again?"
"It's just for a check-up. He wants to listen to your chest. If it's all right then you can go on a holiday to the mountains."
"I'm all right now. I'm much better aren't I?" Dieter liked the sound of a holiday in the mountains. Wait till the children at school heard.

Once through Muersbach they headed towards Losbergsreuth. It was a small hamlet set in a serene part of the countryside. From Zaugendorf it was over eight kilometers each way but they took their time and enjoyed the scenery. As they neared Losbergsreuth they could see the settlement perched on the crest of a hill in the middle of forest. A wagon track wound through the forest and up towards the homes. Here and there they could see it through a break in the trees as it snaked out into a clearing again.
"Let's have a rest." Oma sat down on a seat beside the track. She seemed to be more easily tired these days. Life was certainly busy now that she had her own house to look after. Mind you, it was more convenient as well. A peaceful happy environment!
Dieter sat beside her for all of two minutes and then he was up and fossicking around again. He might be thin but he had all the energy and enthusiasm of a young lad. The trees were sparsely planted at the edge of the forest with room to spread their limbs. Here they did not have to compete for a spot in the sun or fight their way upward through dense foliage. Beech, oak and pine trees swayed in the breeze dappling the sunlight as Dieter bent to smell the lily of the valley. May bells they called them.
"Don't pick them Dieter. They'll only die without water."
"I know Oma, but they smell so beautiful." Dieter breathed in the sweet perfume.

"Let's get going." Oma stood up and they set off once more. Up through Losbergsreuth where they were greeted by friendly people then down through the forest. From here they could see Ebern in the distance stretched out before them. It was a medieval town with the remains of watch-towers and ramparts that history showed had not been needed in this peaceful area of Germany. Over the bridge walked Dieter and Oma, past the stone walls to the arched entrance to the town. The gates had long gone and the settlement was untouched by the ravages of war they had seen in other parts of Germany. The town clock high overhead proclaimed the half hour as the town dwellers bustled about their tasks.

"Eleven thirty. Let's go to the Gasthof before it gets busy. I'm peckish and I guess you are too."

Yes he was, now he thought about it. His tummy was rumbling. Oma ordered a bread roll each with a sausage and mustard.

"A lemonade for the lad and I'll have a coffee please."

After lunch they wended their way through the narrow streets to Dr Stark's rooms. There were no other patients waiting so Dr Stark was able to see them straight away.

"Now what can I do for you today?"

Oma produced the letter and showed it to him.

"Good! At last they've listened to me," the doctor said. "Well young man, let's have a listen to your chest."

Dieter took off his jacket and lifted up his shirt.

"Big breath," said Dr Stark as he plonked the cold stethoscope against Dieter's back. "Good! Turn around. Hmmmmmm! Sounds just fine to me." He filled in a form with the necessary details and handed it to Oma.

"Take this to the Health Office and good luck. I hope you don't have to wait too long."

Down the street they went, round the corner, past the market and into a two-storey building flanking the street. They climbed the stairs. A bell jingled as they opened the door labeled 'Health Office' and went over to the desk.

"We've come to see about this matter."

"I see." The officer muttered to himself as he scanned the letter.

"Good. You've been to the doctor and everything is fine. There is nothing that fresh mountain air, wholesome food and plenty of sunshine won't fix."

"We've done our best!"

"Of course you have but now we want to help. See if we can fatten him up a bit."

Oma smiled. She had tried and it was not that easy.

Finally Oma was handed the papers and a voucher.

"Use the voucher to get Dieter what he needs. There's a list there." He pointed to the papers. "The next intake is in two weeks' time."

As they left Oma felt pleased that it was happening quite quickly. She would go home and talk to Peppi about it, but really it was time Erika helped with her son. Oma loved him dearly but she had four working people in the house now and without Liesl to help with chores she often felt tired. Admittedly Erika was expecting her third child but Christa was almost four and not a baby any more.

The next week it was all arranged. Dieter went to live with Mutti and Christa, in Muersbach. Werner was long gone! After school he enjoyed playing with his little half sister that he hardly knew. While Dieter was at school Mutti went through the list of items required and purchased what was needed. So many things – blue and white striped T-shirts, shorts, leather sandals, shoe cleaner, singlets, undies, pyjamas, a bath robe too, towels, a toilet bag packed with soap in a container, a comb, toothbrush and even toothpaste. All this was packed into a new suitcase. Dieter went through all the contents piece by piece explaining it all to Christa.

"Can I come too?" It all sounded very exciting to her.

"No you can't. I have to go away to the mountains because I've been sick with tuberculosis. The doctor said I must."

Christa nodded. The day before he left Oma came over to say goodbye.

"I know you'll be a good boy. You'll meet lots of new friends and have plenty of milk straight from the cows. They have cows up in the mountains where you're going and they feed on wildflowers all day. The milk is very sweet and will make you strong." She was trying to console herself more than Dieter. So far it was all really exciting for him. Tomorrow he was going on the train.

"It won't be long and then you'll be back." Oma gave him a kiss and left at once. She had cared for him since he was born and they had never been apart before. She knew it was for the best but eight weeks would seem an eternity to both of them. She had no doubt that Dieter would feel homesick with the strangeness of it all when he arrived. Thank goodness he had not cried and clung to her today. So Oma trudged home to cook a meal for her husband and three grown up offspring.

CHAPTER TWENTY-EIGHT

Next morning Dieter was very excited as he dressed in his travel clothes. Mutti was travelling with him to Bamberg and then handing him over to a chaperone to travel on to Fuessen. Christa was to stay with Mrs Reis who lived upstairs.

"You promise to be a good girl for Mutti while I'm away."

"I'm always good. Aren't I Mutti?"

"Yes my sweet." She picked up Dieter's case as Mrs Reis took Christa by the hand.

"See you in eight weeks." Dieter held up eight fingers as Christa turned and he left to catch the train.

Mutti carried the suitcase as Dieter pattered along beside her on the way to the station. He held his lunch in a paper bag. He had never had a packed lunch before and he felt quite grown up, like Opa, Heinz and Rudi going off to work. It was ages since he had been on a train too. They had not been waiting long, just long enough for Mutti to stop panting when the train huffed and puffed into Hilgersdorf Station. My, it was big and powerful. They climbed into the carriage and Mutti stowed his case on the overhead rack. Dieter settled himself on the seat by the window. Soon they were on their way to Bamberg, hurtling through the undulating countryside, past clusters of houses and clumps of trees, through fields with new spring growth sprouting. Dieter sat in silence surveying the scenery, thinking about the adventure he was embarking on. Part of him was excited – new clothes, a train ride up into the mountains – but part of him was hesitant. He would be on his own without any family. He was used to living life without his mother, but Oma, Opa and Rudi…….. What would life be like without them? In all his eight years he had never spent a night alone.

Mutti sat beside him with her hands clasped over her pregnant belly. She was deep in her own thoughts. How would she manage with a second child to care for? Thank goodness her mother was looking after Dieter. Some of his expressions reminded her of Max, but she did not want to think about him. There was no doubt about it she had had bad luck with her men, could not seem to hold them. It was all very well for them to get what they wanted and clear off. All the fun and no responsibility! People in the village did not seem to understand. She knew they talked behind her back. Often a group of women chatting would stop and watch silently as she walked past. But she would show them she could manage. She was tired of all the arguments, all the excuses why the men had to move on. They could all get lost, she would do things her way. Who needed a man anyway?

"Are we nearly there?"

"My goodness, I believe we are."

The spire of Bamberg Dome could be seen above the skyline. Built over one thousand years ago the yellow stone edifice was still standing tall. Once they were on the station Mutti looked around for a matronly figure with children clustered around her. She was the one to take all the children onto Fuessen near the Austrian border. Mutti held Dieter's hand firmly. Ah, there they were. A group of children wearing name tags and all holding hands.

"Mrs Klier?" the woman asked.

"Yes." Mutti was not about to explain the facts of the matter, it was none of her business.

"And you must be Dieter."

Dieter gave her a shy smile.

"Well we'd better get on board now everybody's here." Mutti filed along behind with Dieter's suitcase. They all clambered into the nearest carriage and she put Dieter's luggage on the rack beside that of the other children.

"Goodbye Son." Mutti gave him a quick peck on the cheek. "See you in eight weeks. Now be a good boy."

"Yes Mutti." He felt quite bereft as he looked around at the others.

"My name is Fraulein Herta and you can sit next to me."

Dieter sat down beside her. An older boy sitting opposite gave him a wink.

"We're going to the mountains." Dieter nodded. "The cat got your tongue?" Dieter looked at Fraulein Herta. There was no cat here. What was she talking about? And anyway cats did not go around collecting little boys' tongues. A smile crossed his face.

"No I kept my mouth shut so that it couldn't."

Fraulein Herta laughed. "That's good then."

As they left Bamberg and the train settled into a rocking rhythm Fraulein Herta told them all to look out for mountains, lakes and castles.

"It's very beautiful where we're going. See who can spot them first."

They stopped at stations along the way until in the end Fraulein Herta was responsible for twenty children. They were all sitting together and she paired older children with the younger ones. Some were quiet and withdrawn while others chatted excitedly. Fear radiated from the big brown eyes of a little girl sitting on the other side of Fraulein Herta. Dieter leaned forward and gave her a smile. It was dim on their side of the train but the sun shone brightly over the countryside. The rolling country near Bamberg gave way to flat land as they went through Munich and headed further south.

"See those mountains? That's where we're going."

Dieter peered through the smoke streaked window. In the distance he could see mountains rising out of the land, their snow capped peaks standing out against a blue sky.

"Let's have our lunch now and then we can spot the lakes and castles." Fraulein Herta helped the younger children unwrap their lunches. Mmmmm! Dieter breathed in the smell of fresh baked bread. Thick slices of dark bread spread with butter and jam. He was tempted to open up the sandwiches and lick the jam off first but decided against it. Helmut from school said only babies did that.

A vague memory from the past stirred in Dieter, a memory of being stuffed in a carriage with Oma and Opa. It was very cramped and there was no food. He looked around him. Here no one was standing and they all had food. But they were all strangers that he had never seen before. Fraulein Herta was gazing out the window contemplating, enjoying the near silence while her charges ate. Dieter could see a thick slice of sausage sticking out of her sandwich, but jam was just as good. He opened his bottle of cocoa and took a swig. Mutti made good cocoa, with sugar. The sweet chocolate flavour oozed down his throat and he continued eating.

"Put the top back on, Dieter. We don't want it to spill, do we?"

"Yes Fraulein." Of course he did not want to waste even a drop. He gazed out the window as he munched on. The mountains seemed to be growing bigger now, the snow lit up by the sun. He could see rocky outcrops breaking through here and there. Trees stood together as though deep in conversation. What was that? Something shone out like a mirror from a nearby stand of trees, Dieter looked again. It must be a lake. How beautiful was that?

"Look Fraulein, a lake."

"So it is. Well done Dieter. That must be Starnberg Lake."

All the children craned to see.

"Mind your lunches. If any fall on the floor we'll have to throw them out."

Dieter watched as they drew closer. The silver reflection turned to blue. Not a ripple ruffled the surface. It was nothing like the River Itz that burbled its way through Zaugendorf. This was serene and still. He imagined what it would be like in a boat, floating on the stillness. Dieter woke from his reverie. He had finished his sandwich, now for the rest of his cocoa.

The huge, rocky mountains seemed to be moving closer towards them. He could see their feet poking out through the trees now. All he could hear though was the clackety-clack of the train. At last the mountains had come right up to them and the train slowed down and crept into the station with a slow hisssss. FUESSEN it said on the signboard. Here they were at last.

"Now get all your things. Don't leave anything behind. What about your jacket, Franz? You'd better put it on. It could be cool out there."

Fraulein Herta bustled about as she lifted suitcases down onto the seats. She organised the older boys to take them to the carriage door where the station attendant swung them down onto a trolley. You could tell she had made this trip many times before.

"Hold your partner's hand!"

That's a bit silly, thought Dieter. How can we get down the steps like that! Eventually everyone was off the train and their luggage stood beside them.

"Is that everyone?" The stationmaster was used to these groups coming through Fuessen. He smiled to himself as Fraulein Herta counted heads.

"Yes that's all thank you. Now come along children. We need to wait for the bus." The line of children led by their chaperone wound down the road that ran past the station where a bus was waiting for them. The driver stowed all the bags in the racks overhead and then the children piled in.

"We're off. Won't be long now." The bus rattled and bumped its way through birches and fruit trees lining the route. Meadows stretched out beyond the trees and then they saw a chalet on the side of the mountain. It was three storeys tall and the roof had a steep pitch to allow the snow to slide off in winter. It was a big building crouching there under its roof.

Dieter stretched and yawned as he got off the bus. A woman in nurse's uniform bustled out to meet them. She wore a sky blue dress with a white apron over the top. Sitting on her head was a white hat which looked as though it was too small for her but was held firmly in place with hair clips. Everything about her was neat and in order.

"Welcome children. I hope you've had a good trip." Most nodded glumly.

"Come in and we'll unpack and help you to put your things away."

She took them through the front door where a gleaming corridor showed the way to the stairs.

"You're all on the top floor."

Clump, clump, clump! Twenty pairs of little feet bore their owners up three flights of stairs. Up and round, up and round, up and round again. Phew! A long corridor ran the length of the top floor separating the boys' dormitory from the girls. Dieter was ushered into a room where two nurses were waiting to greet them. A wall with a door in it divided the dormitory into two rooms – one for the older boys and one for the younger ones. A contingent of staff helped the big boys with the luggage. Once his suitcase had arrived Dieter was assigned a bed and began to unpack his things like the boy next door was doing.

"Put your towel on the end of your bed, dear. The rest goes in the cupboard." She pointed to a set of drawers beside his bed. It didn't take long to unpack and get everything ship shape.

"My name is Sister Johanna and this is Sister Maria." Sister Johanna's eyes smiled as she spoke in a kindly voice. Sister Maria looked on with her arms folded. "We're here to look after you but first we need to show you around. This is the boys' dormitory and across the corridor is the girls' dormitory which is out of bounds to you. Do you understand that?"

"Yes Sister Maria," they chorused.

"Good, then let's go downstairs."

The second floor was set up like the third. More dormitories with a corridor down the middle.

"Now the first floor." This is where they had entered when they arrived.

"This is the kitchen." Dieter could smell delicious aromas emanating from there. Food was on its way. "No children allowed!"

Behind it was the dining room. Tall windows let in the last of the sun before it sank behind the mountains.

"And these are the boys' toilets. The girls' are on the other side of the passage." Sister Johanna ushered them in to have a look.

"So there you are. That's about all you need to know. You'll soon get used to the routine and what to do when."

Sister Maria looked at her watch. "My goodness, it's almost time for dinner. Let's have a quick look outside but please stay together. We don't want anyone lost and missing out on dinner, do we?"

The air was clean and crisp outside with shadows lengthening on the edges. There was a wide open space behind the Home with enormous rocks covered in lichens and moss near a stand of pine trees and silver birches down the end of the building. Sister Johanna clapped her hands.

"Right children, time to get washed for dinner."

They re-entered the Home and went to the bathroom to wash their hands. Ding-dong went the speakers overhead.

"That's the first bell for dinner. Let's go and find our places." Sister Maria took them into the dining room.

"These are your seats so every time you come to eat, this is where you'll sit. Over there is the servery where you line up when it's your turn."

It was a large room with rows of tables but they still needed two sittings for each meal. The third floor was the first sitting. Dieter was thankful for that. It seemed ages ago since he had eaten lunch on the train. When the second bell sounded Sister Johanna ushered Dieter's table up to the servery. Dieter's eyes grew large as he took the plate offered to him. Very carefully he took it back to his place and set it down. He had potatoes smothered with quark perched on the edge of the plate. The rest was taken up with a delicious smelling, rich stew dotted with cauliflower and carrots. At home Oma needed to make that amount of meat stretch around the whole family. It seemed too good to be true and it tasted as good as it smelled. When they were all finished, back to the servery they went with their dirty plates to pick up the second course – a thick creamy custard and fruit. My, oh my! This was fantastic food. Then Sister Johanna brought round a tray of mugs filled with hot chocolate to finish off the meal. Dieter thought he might burst but he felt duty bound not to let Oma down. Did she know it was going to be like this? She must have!

Finally it was off to the toilet on the way upstairs and get ready for bed. It seemed strange with so many boys in one room. Sisters Johanna and Maria supervised, showing children how to fold their clothes neatly and put them in their lockers with their shoes side by side underneath. Dieter smelt his new pyjamas before he put them on. They were thick and fluffy after Mutti had washed them. He wondered what she was doing tonight. And what about Oma and Opa? Were they missing him? As he snuggled in to bed a tear or two rolled out onto his pillow. The lights overhead were turned off and dim night lights took their turn, shedding a pale glow over the room. "Good night children. Sleep well."

The nurses began to sing to the children. More tears fell onto Dieter's pillow as he listened to the lullaby that Oma often sang to him. "Abends wenn ich schlafen geh,

Vierzehn Engle um mich stehen......."

It wasn't long before the effects of the long journey, a good meal and maybe the fourteen angels had their way and Dieter drifted off to sleep.

CHAPTER TWENTY-NINE

The next morning Dieter woke up as Sister Maria moved through the dormitory and opened the curtains. He stretched and looked at the sun streaming in.

"Time to get up children. We're having showers before breakfast." Sister Maria's voice cut across his thoughts.

"That's the boy. Put on your bathrobe and slippers. Do you remember where the bathroom is?"

Dieter nodded. It was taking him a while to wake up but then he thought if breakfast is half as good as dinner last night it would be well worth the effort. Sister Maria stood in the middle of the room and clapped her hands.

"Right children, this is Sister Herta. When you're all ready she will show you to the bathroom. Take your towels and toilet bags."

Sister Herta was lovely. She was buxom and smiled at the faces of twenty little boys gazing solemnly at her. She seemed more relaxed than she'd been on the train yesterday.

"All ready? Come along then."

They shuffled out of the room and down the stairs to the bathroom.

"Hang your bathrobes here and put your slippers underneath. That's the way."

Dieter wrapped his arms around himself and looked at all the naked bodies.

"First your teeth and then into the shower."

They moved over to a long line of basins against the wall to do her bidding. Dieter was shivering so cleaned his teeth as quickly as possible before hopping into a shower. It was luxurious. A row of showers stretched along the opposite wall with no partitions. Sister Herta tested the water for him.

"Soap yourself well and be quick. There are lots of children to get through."

Everything ran like clockwork. Soon Dieter joined the line of hungry children scampering down the stairs. He walked beside a little girl who looked shy and unsure of herself.

"I wonder what we'll have for breakfast."

"Mm," was all she said. Her eyes were red and her face blotchy as though she had been crying.

"It's bound to be good if it's like dinner last night."

It was! Big beakers brimming with fresh frothy milk from the cows, thick slices of bread slathered with butter and grated cheese packed on top and a bowl of peeled hard-boiled eggs on the table. All ready waiting to be eaten.

"Would you like some more?"

Dieter had big eyes but his stomach was not used to so much food.

"No thank you." He knew he would not go hungry here.

After breakfast they were given free time to go and play outside. Dieter wandered across the meadows and picked wildflowers, looking around for the sad little girl. She was standing over by the building all alone.

"These are for you." He held out the flowers. "What's your name? My name's Dieter. Come and help me pick some more. We can give them to the sisters."

Anna brightened up and together they picked a big bunch. Dieter gave some to Sister Johanna and Anna gave hers to the sister looking after her.

Next came exercise time – flopping down like rag dolls, touching toes then slowly rolling up again; swaying from side to side with arms held aloft like tall trees in the wind; star jumps with arms and legs wide and then together; arms reaching out in front of them, then hands brought into the chest and elbows stretched out to the side. It was hard work but after a short rest they continued. Just as well he didn't have any more breakfast. In time he would get used to it. Finally Sister Martha called a halt. She was older than the other sisters but tall and thin. Each day she would be in charge of the exercise programme.

"Next Monday we will go for a hike instead. Not too far. It's a surprise so I'm not telling you where."

The sisters who had been standing around the outside organized their groups into a game of leap frog.

"Make sure you come in when you hear the lunch bell."

"Yes Sister." Exercise out in the mountain air had used up all his breakfast and Dieter for one would not be tardy when the bell sounded.

Lunch! More bread with thick butter, mustard and sliced sausages and cold meats. Yummee! Wait till he told Rudi about this. Would he believe him? Next came fresh fruit – bananas, apples, pears, plums or oranges. Never had Dieter seen so much food and such variety since they left Czechoslovakia and that was a long time ago now. After lunch it was time to have a sleep. Later on they often went for a walk before dinner and so the days rolled on.

Sundays were different. On Sunday the priest came to say Mass and a Lutheran pastor came too. Dieter went to the Lutheran service as his father was Lutheran, Oma said. The liturgy reminded him of the Catholic Mass a little but the pastor did not seem so foreboding. After church it was free time till lunch, then a sleep. Some things did not change even on a Sunday. Mind you, Dieter usually had a sleep with Opa on Sunday afternoons before coffee and cake with their friends.

When the children woke from their sleep on fine Sundays they often had entertainment by the older children. Running along by the dining room were clumps of pine trees and silver birch with huge rocks jutting out in between. They were wonderful for playing hide and seek on other days – if you were smart you could sidle round the rock to stay hidden from your "seeker". But on Sundays the young ones sat on the grass in front while the older children used the layout of the rocks to form an ampitheatre and put on a play. They had few props but they were such fun to watch. The stories they told were old Germanic tales and legends that the children knew. Dieter laughed loudly when a boy crouching down with a green cloth over him hopped out as they re-enacted the story of the frog prince. At times like that he became lost in the moment and forgot about his loved ones at home.

Some children received letters from home and Anna even got a packet with biscuits and a new ribbon for her hair. How Dieter wished something would be there for him when Sister Maria handed out letters after the evening meal on mail days. But every time he was disappointed. He watched sadly as he saw the joy on other children's faces when they tore open a letter from home. It had happened so often that now Dieter used to gaze out the window into the dark night and dream of home instead of watching the children. He thought about Oma cooking the evening meal and Opa, Heinz and Rudi trudging home from work. Christa was probably getting ready for bed. And what about Helmut? Was he missing him at school?

"Dieter here's something for you!" He came to with a start to see Sister Maria beaming as she held out a letter. Dieter scurried over to collect it.

"Thank you Sister Maria! Thank you so much." It seemed as though she had organized it.

"That's all right. It's from your mother."

Dieter ripped open the envelope but it was difficult to read with blurry eyes. He blinked once, twice, ah, that was better.

Dear Dieter,

How are you? I hope you are well and getting strong. Christa misses you and keeps asking when you are coming home. We went over to see Oma and Opa the other day and they both send their love. Opa's garden is coming on fine now. He gave me some carrots and beetroot to bring home. They are delicious! Oma had a vase of flowers on the dresser. From her own garden. Asters and roses – just beautiful.

Well I must go and cook Christa's dinner. Be a good boy. I love you. I'm thinking of you.

Love Mutti

PS Next time I'll send you a packet.

Dieter looked around the dining room as he drank his cocoa. You could tell who had letters and who did not. He knew what it felt like to be disappointed. Before he went to sleep that night he breathed in the smell of his letter as he tucked it under his pillow. It smelled of Mutti and somehow brought his family closer to him.

True to her word about two weeks later Mutti sent him a packet. It was very well wrapped and he needed help from Sister Johanna to cut the string and get into it. He could not believe his eyes. Biscuits made by Mutti and a bar of chocolate. He had never had one all to himself before. He breathed in the aroma, then again more deeply.

Although he had just finished dinner he managed to find space for half the chocolate bar and shared biscuits with a boy on each side of him. He felt strange as he climbed into bed later. Mutti had sent him a packet and he had been very excited when he realized it was for him. But now he just wanted to go home. He missed them all more than ever. He clutched the wrapping paper in his hand and held it to his nose as the tears spilled over.

"What's wrong, Honey?" asked Sister Johanna.

"I miss my Oma."

Sister Johanna stroked his head as she began to sing a song. His eyes slowly closed with tears still glistening on his eyelashes.

CHAPTER THIRTY

Another special day they went for a hike instead of doing exercises at the Home. They took their lunch with them.

"Where are we going?"

"Oh, that's to be a nice surprise."

They set off in pairs in a long line. Sister Maria led the train with Sister Herta in the middle and Sister Johanna bringing up the rear. The path wound through the meadow and Dieter picked flowers as he went, wandering off the path to gaze about him.

"Come Dieter. We have to stay together."

"These are for you." He held the bunch out to Sister Johanna.

"Thank you. But now we'll have to walk fast and catch up." She took his hand and they hurried along to the end of the line. The track took them round towards the mountains then skirted along the side. They passed two men working in a granite quarry, chipping out the greyish black granite for monuments and gravestones.

"Nice day for a walk," one called.

"Yes, but it's a surprise where we're going," Dieter replied.

"Well, don't get lost or you won't find out."

Dieter skipped along. The birds sang and so did Sister Johanna.

"I love to go a-wandering
Along a mountain track
And as I go I love to sing,
My knapsack on my back."

She turned to show Dieter her knapsack. He laughed. As they rounded a bend there was a crystal clear mountain stream gurgling over rocks and pebbles. Some of the children were already sitting down, taking off their socks and shoes.

"Right! Off with your clothes and into the stream."

Brrr! It was cold.

"Lie down on your tummies with your hands out in front of you," Sister Herta instructed. "That's right Anna. Good girl. Now put your face down in the water and count to ten. Raise your head when you need a breath."

At first the cold water almost took his breath away but once he was used to it Dieter was reluctant to get out.

"Everybody out!" The nurses beckoned from the other side of the stream. They busied themselves drying the children off with towels from their knapsacks. The children were rubbed down briskly.

"Now into your clothes again."

As they set off once more the path became narrower leading them upwards beside a rock wall. Here they had to go in single file holding hands. Two planks were fastened into the rock wall with a cable used for a handrail. At last they came to the top, feeling safe once more. A locked gate confronted them.

"Yoohoo! Is there someone there to let us in?"

High up on the parapet of the fairytale castle in front of them a voice replied. A man came down and choosing a key from his large bunch he unlocked a small side gate.

"This way!"

My word this was beautiful. A real castle. Neuschwanstein. The turrets with little windows shone brightly in the sunshine. Tiles capped each turret like the paper cones the children got when they started school. Dieter's mouth hung open as they were ushered through and into the entrance hall and on into the castle. Paintings on the walls, gilded with gold, chandeliers hung from the ceilings. Ornately carved dressers were adorned with candelabra. The throne room was impressive with lapis lazuli and gold everywhere he looked. Dieter would have liked to try out the throne to see what it felt like to be a king but there was no throne there. Anyway God the judge looked down from a painting above the empty dais. The twelve apostles watched from the other walls. It was all so magnificent. What a wonderful surprise this had been. Wait till he told the children at school, Oma and Opa and Rudi too, Christa and Mutti. He had been inside King Ludwig's castle, one of the homes of the King of Bavaria. It was awe inspiring and the children were hushed as they tiptoed through.

Finally they filed through the expansive kitchen and out into the brilliant sunshine in the courtyard. Tables were set out with milk, bread, sausage, cheese and fruit. Dieter looked around. Yes! Now that he thought about it he was very hungry. The children sat around on benches and tucked in. As the children finished they sat against the sun-warmed stone walls and sang songs together while they waited for the others. Once the tables were cleared army stretchers were brought out into the courtyard for the children to have an afternoon nap.

"No talking!" they were told. After the walk in the mountain air and dip in the stream most of the children succumbed to sleep. What did they dream of? Probably knights on horses come to rescue fairy princesses from fiery dragons, or some such thing.

By mid-afternoon it was time to head home once more, back down the mountain. Only this time they took off their sandals and waded through the stream. Back at the Kinderheim there was excited chatter as the children washed up for their evening meal. They sat down to potatoes, capped with quark like the mountain tops in winter, and a ghoulash of meat and vegetables followed by custard and fruit. What a splendid day it had been. It would have been perfect if Oma had been there.

Time at the Kinderheim had seemed to stretch out forever when Dieter first arrived. There had been episodes of homesickness and other times that he was bursting to share with his family. Soon he would be doing that. But first he must be measured and weighed for the records.

"My word, you've grown and put on weight." Dieter beamed. Oma would be pleased.

The group from the south of Munich set out on the return journey with Sister Herta once more. Only this time they knew where they were going. Home to tell everyone about it! Dieter hummed to himself as he sat in the train and watched the world go by. Villages, fields with crops and animals, children waving and people eagerly waiting on stations. The number of children in the carriage began to dwindle and Dieter swapped seats to sit next to Sister Herta. This time he was not apprehensive, but excited.

"Looking forward to seeing your family again?"

"Yes I am."

"What will you tell them?"

"Oh, everything, they'll want to know everything."

"I'm sure they will. What did you like best?"

"The food! And the castle! That's what I liked best."

Sister Herta smiled and nodded. Next they would be arriving in Bamberg and his mother would be there to meet them. Dieter pressed his face to the window as the train pulled in. He scanned the faces looking for his mother.

"Mutti! There she is."

Sister Herta picked up his suitcase and they climbed down from the train as Mutti hurried over.

"Look at you, just look at you!" she beamed as she planted a kiss on his cheek. "You've put on weight and you're brown as a berry." She looked at Sister Herta. "Thank you so much for your care. He looks well and strong now." She pinched Dieter's cheek.

"Yes the good food and mountain air makes a difference all right. So goodbye Mrs Klier and good luck Dieter." She waved as she clambered back on the train to her other charges. They all waved to Dieter as he turned his back and took Mutti's hand to find their train to Muersbach. Frequently between Bamberg and Muersbach Mutti smiled at Dieter and pinched his cheeks again. He wished she would stop but she was obviously pleased to see him so he said nothing.

"When will I see Oma and Opa?"

"Tomorrow. I'll take you back tomorrow."

It would be good to see Christa but he really missed Opa and Oma. He would be living with them again. He breathed a sigh of relief.

CHAPTER THIRTY-ONE

Soon after Dieter's return from the Kinderheim it was summer holidays. No sooner had he recounted his wonderful tales of life in the mountains than it seemed another holiday had arrived. Some of the time Dieter stayed with Mutti and Christa in Muersbach and the rest of the time he stayed with Opa and Oma in Zaugendorf. Oma was always tired these days although she never complained. Being near the end of her pregnancy, Mutti was always tired too. At least he had Christa to play with or the boys from school when he grew sick of her games.

It was a lovely day in Muersbach. A group of boys sauntered down the street in front of their house and Dieter joined them.
"Where are you going?"
"Down to the creek. Want to come?"
"Yes, I'll just tell my mother."
So off they went to sail bark boats down the creek.
"Look there's Otto."
Otto ambled towards them with a grin on his face. He was much older than them with fuzz on his top lip and round his cheeks. They called him silly Otto. His usual task was to carry water or fetch firewood for some of the women in the village. He might be simple but he was strong and always obedient.
"Want to play?" Fritz, the leader of the group asked.
Otto grinned and nodded.
"Come on then, we're going to the creek." They'd learned from past experience that if you wanted to have some fun at Otto's expense you needed to move away from the houses so that you could not be seen or heard.

Down near the creek they gathered round Otto while he stood and grinned at them still.
"We're going to sail boats. Want to help?"

He grunted and nodded agreement.

"Let's go then, but first we want to see you jump."

The smile faded from his face and his eyes flicked from one to the other.

"Jump Otto."

Obligingly he jumped. His big bare feet thumped and his stomach wobbled under his shirt as he landed. The children laughed.

"Higher Otto, jump higher," another boy joined in. There was no doubt that he was a good jumper. He was tall and strong in spite of his disability.

"Jump Otto, jump." Again and again he jumped. He wiped the snot from his nose with the back of his hand. He began to grunt each time he landed, his shorts shivering with each impact of his sturdy man's legs on the dry earth.

"Again Otto!" Now he was crying in his deep man's voice and the children fell about laughing. He looked like a man yet he was not. No one else in the village could amuse them like Otto. He just did what they said and the children reveled in the power they had over him.

"Just once more. Jump!" Otto was breathing heavily now and they could smell the sweat pouring off him. Suddenly a shadow fell across the circle and the group froze. It was Otto's mother. "What is happening here?" she asked. In a gentler voice she called, "Come Otto." She put her arm across his shoulder as she wiped his face with a handkerchief. "Wait till your parents hear about this!"

Silence fell as they watched her lead Otto away. Dieter was concerned. Mutti lived in the flat below Otto's, rented it from Otto's mother. There would be no getting away from this one. He wandered away from the boys and followed the creek along. Now he felt a chill in the air. He kicked stones as he went, crossing the bridge and meandering along the path. The day was ruined with a cloud hanging over him. Why had he taken part in the fiasco, making fun of Otto? He would never do it again, not that Mutti would take any notice of that today. Ahead of him across the meadows he spied Christof's hut. Christof looked after goats from the village. Each day he called them as he walked through with his own goats and flock of geese. He was an older man and Dieter had enjoyed many hours with him. That is where he would go to fill in time and put off the evil hour.

Christof's hut was an A-frame shelter built of logs. A bench ran along each side with a table in the middle.

"Why so glum on such a beautiful day?"

Dieter hung his head. "I'm in trouble. We were getting Otto to jump and his mother caught us."

"Well, you'll have to face the music when you get home."

"I know."

Christof took a pinch of tobacco from his pouch and sniffed it up his nose. This was the one thing about Christof that Dieter did not like. Such a lovely gentle man but with such a dirty habit. Not that he ever said anything about it. Christof continued whittling in silence.

"What's that you're making today?" Dieter asked.

"Another whistle. Would you like it?"

"Yes please. I gave the other one to Christa when I went away. She likes to play it."

"Good. Then I'll show you how to play a new song."

Dieter watched as he carefully crafted the mouthpiece with reeds that grew by the river and fitted it in place. He played a few notes to test it.

"Yes, it'll do." He began to play *At the well by the gate*. Dieter marveled at his dexterous fingers that carved such a whistle and then produced a lilting song. He clapped when Christof finished.

"That's better. Here, you play this one and I'll play mine. Then you can see how it goes."

"Thank you." He took the whistle in his hands and held it with care, his eyes smiling again.

Christof showed Dieter the fingering and how to avoid producing a squeak. Phrase by phrase Dieter watched the music master, adding each onto the tail of the last until he had it pat. The time flew until it was time to go home.

"The day's not so bad when you put some music in it, is it?"

"No it's not."

"Remember we all have choices – to brighten up the day or cause sorrow. It's up to you."

"Yes, I'll try."

"Remember you've done wrong so go home and face it like a man."

Dieter hung his head. "Yes Christof."

"That's my boy!" he patted his head and gave him a gentle push in the direction of home.

With hands in his pockets and head down, Dieter set off. It was all very well for Christof to say that but he did not know what the punishment would be. Dieter had never talked about it with the other children but he suspected that no one else was beaten with an electric cord. He hoped Mutti had not replaced it after Opa had taken the last one home in his bag.

CHAPTER THIRTY-TWO

Although deep winter had passed it was still cold on the way to and from school. Dieter plunged his hands into his jacket pockets and hunched over against the biting wind, deep in thought. Today Father Schugmann had been at school. He had talked with the class about first Holy Communion. Dieter had just turned nine.

"Such a privilege but you'll need to work hard," he said. "Classes will start next week. Take this home to your parents." He handed a note to each child.

Dieter fingered the note in his pocket. He had watched the excitement build up for older children in the school and the pride on their parents' faces on the day. Would Opa and Oma come to church that day? If they didn't surely Mutti would.

Round the table that evening Opa picked up the note and read it. "What's this?" A frown crossed his face. Oma said nothing.

"Well I suppose it's got to be. Can't have you standing out like a sore thumb!"

It was expected, no questions asked. There was only one school in the village and only one church. So preparations began. At school the children were drilled in the catechism. Thank goodness I've got a good memory, Dieter thought, or I'd have raw knuckles. Helmut was not so lucky.

On Saturday Opa was busy in his shed all morning. Dieter wondered what he was doing but Opa did not care for any chatterboxes that day. Dieter helped Oma instead, carrying water from the well and bringing in more firewood.

"You're a great help. What would I do without you?" Oma was sitting down having a rest while a cake cooked. Opa appeared in the doorway.

"Here you are," he beamed. "A box for you to collect things."

"Oh, Opa, thank you." He ran his hands along the leather straps that would hold it on his back. It was made of wood and sturdy.

"Here try it on." Dieter slipped his arms through the straps while Opa held it.

"Well how about that! Just right."

"Can I go now?"

"Yes but just around here. Lunch in an hour."

Oma patted his head and sighed as he went out the door. She worried how things would go for him if she was no longer around. Now she was unable to do the shopping and relied on her Pepi to do it on his way home from work. He never complained but she could see that he was worried too.

"Erika can do the baking. It's too much for you."

Oma nodded.

"I know," she whispered.

Dieter set off down the road. He knew what to do, he had seen some of the others collecting things for their first Holy Communion celebration. Not everyone needed to do it, mainly the refugees. He knocked on Kathi's door.

"Do you have anything to spare for my first Holy Communion?"

"Why, of course. Come in." Kathi went to the cool basement under the house and loaded eggs and freshly churned butter into his wooden knapsack.

"Now you'll need sugar too and some jam. I'll just put them under the eggs."

"Oh thank you. You will come to the feast, won't you?"

"I'd love to, Dieter. Now you go home carefully and unpack those eggs first."

"Yes Kathi." Dieter headed home and proudly showed Oma the ingredients. She placed them carefully in a big basket.

"Opa can take these to your mother. She is going to bake all the fine things for your celebration."

Dieter set off again. First to the Kleinleins and then to the Matthes. Everyone in Zaugendorf knew Dieter as he had eaten in every house at some time or another. Nuts, cream, flour, spices - whatever was on offer he accepted with a smile and a thank you.

"Lunch time now. So wash your hands." Dieter felt really hungry when he thought about what Mutti would be able to bake. In a flash he obeyed and sat at the table. Oma ladled soup into bowls and Opa set them on the table. Thick slabs of bread were used for dunking.

"So what's the plan for this afternoon?" Opa smiled across the table.

"I haven't been to Funks, Seppels or Oppels yet."

"See how you go. That might be enough."

After lunch Dieter continued. Over the next week after school he went to other houses, giving everyone the opportunity to help out. Whenever his box was full he went back to Oma to unload.

"I think fourteen houses are enough." Opa called a halt. "You'll have to help me get it to your mother because I haven't got a truck."

Not that Dieter minded. He was looking forward to the feast – just like the wedding.

In the meantime Mutti and Liesel were busy making a dark suit for Dieter - long trousers and a jacket.

"My word, you'll look smart."

"Like Heinz and Gerti's wedding, Opa."

"Yes."

Next Mutti started baking. She stretched dough out on large flat cake trays and curled the edges over the jam and streusel strewn on top. More dough was pulled into shape over a clean tea towel on her knee then dropped into a pan of hot lard. Dieter watched as deftly she scooped them out with a sieve and sprinkled icing sugar over them. Cakes were made and cooked in the landlady's oven. Everything was stored in paper lined suitcases on the top shelf. Dieter's mouth watered just thinking about it. This celebration was for him and nothing could spoil it.

CHAPTER THIRTY-THREE

At last everything was ready and all he had to do was wait. Then it happened. On Sunday, a week before the big day Oma took sick. Visitors had been there for afternoon coffee and kuchen. When they left Oma felt really unwell and went to lie down. Dieter was concerned because Oma never lay down in the daytime. Opa on Sundays, yes, but not Oma. The ambulance was called and Oma was taken to Bamberg Hospital.

"Just till she's better," consoled Opa. Dieter nodded with tears poised to roll down his cheeks. There was nothing else for it. Dieter would need to stay with Mutti while Oma was in hospital. A chill descended over his heart as Rudi and Dieter set off for Muersbach.

"It won't be long!" Rudi gave Dieter and his two little sisters a hug before going out the door again. A final wave and he was gone, into the cold night air.

Sometimes Dieter forgot about his anxiety for Oma. Everyone said she would soon be home and when he was playing with the other children at school he did not remember. But then, after school when he wended his way home to Mutti and the girls it flooded back into his consciousness. Christa would soon be starting school and they could play together but Ingrid was only a toddler. She was a beautiful little girl but with Mutti so busy he needed to help look after her. It would not be forever. Sunday was his big celebration and he hoped Oma would be home by then.

It was not to be. On Thursday Opa trudged in and Dieter could see he had been crying. He sat down and drew Dieter onto his knee.

"Your Oma has died. She's gone from us now Dieterle."

"No, no. I want to see her."

"I know. She was very sick. The doctors couldn't help her. She's at peace now."

"But you said…."

"Yes I thought she'd come home to us again."
Dieter buried his face on Opa's shoulder and clung to him tightly. Together they cried for the one who meant everything to them, the one who had travelled on without them.

On Saturday afternoon Dieter wandered through Muersbach all alone. He had no thought of where he was going but his feet led him to the church. He looked into the church through the heavy doors. It was resplendent in all the trappings for tomorrow's celebration only he did not feel like celebrating now. Oma was dead! He moved past the church and there was the little stone building. The door was ajar so he pushed it open and walked in. With a shock he saw a dark coffin on a bier. He should have known – that was Oma in her coffin. An older woman sat beside it. Her name was Gretl and she always tended people after they died. Her hands were clasped over her apron, her hair streaked with white was pulled back in a bun. Kindly, gently she beckoned to Dieter.
"Would you like to see Oma?"
Dieter said nothing. Slowly he backed out, his eyes moving between Gretl and the cold hard coffin. He was afraid and no he did not want Gretl to raise the lid. Maybe then he would be unable to control his sadness. Gretl nodded kindly as Dieter turned and ran. He went down to the stream and sat on a rock, throwing stones into the water. What would Oma look like now? Her smile would be gone, the smile that made her eyes twinkle, the laughter that made her tummy wobble. Gone forever.

Next day Dieter went alone to his first Holy Communion. That afternoon was to be Oma's funeral. The rest of the family waited at Mutti's place as they solemnly prepared the food and set the tables. Neighbours loaned chairs and crockery. Dieter felt numb as he went through the motions of everything he had learned by rote. He looked at the crucifix standing on the altar. He smelt the incense as the smoke wafted in front of him. He opened his mouth to receive the wafer from Father Schugmann. He felt like a clockwork toy wound up for the occasion. Then it was over and the children began to file out.

Dieter stood aside to let the others past him. One of the altar boys took the processional cross from the side of the altar – the cross used for funerals with black and silver ornamentation entwined below a silver skull. Dieter looked around. What was going on?

Father Schugmann came out of the sacristy wearing his black robe and silver stole. As he walked past the altar he donned his black three-cornered hat and followed the altar boy holding the funeral cross aloft. Other boys carried the censer and incense, the holy water and bells. It could mean only one thing – Oma's funeral was about to begin. The large bell in the belfry had not tolled to announce the rite. There on the plaza outside the church was her coffin on the bier. Did Opa know? He had said it would be this afternoon. Weaving between the well-wishers and ladies that stooped to pinch his cheeks, Dieter darted off down the steps and raced along the path.

"Oma's funeral. It's now. Her coffin's outside the church." It took a while for the family to understand as he panted and gasped out the news.

With that he turned round and ran back to the church. Someone needed to be with Oma and it would take a while for the adults to get there. The priest followed by the whole procession was at the gate by the time Dieter returned. He walked behind Oma's coffin, a small solitary weeping mourner and stood at the foot of the grave.

"In omine patri, et filio, et spiritu sanctus," Father Schugmann made the sign of the cross. "Oremus." Everyone bowed their heads. "Pater noster, qui es in cealis, sanctificetur nome tuum. Adveniat regnum tuum. Fiat voluntastua, sicut in caelo et in terra…"

Dieter came to with a start. Whump! The first shovel of earth hit the coffin as Opa and the rest of the family arrived. Dieter was appalled. Oma was down there and they were tossing dirt into the yawning chasm. He cried until he felt his heart would burst. He hid his face in Opa's coat and put his hands over his ears to block it all out. They must not do this to his Oma! He looked over to the huge stone cross that stood at the edge of the cemetery. Look what people did to Jesus! He suffered too. In a strange way he took comfort that Oma was not alone in this injustice.

"Come Dieter." Rudi took his hand. "Let's go."

Dieter slowly turned and left with the family – Opa, Rudi, Liesel, Heinz and Gerti, Mutti, Onkel Franz and Tante Else Doerre and Onkel Franz Klier! They did not notice when Dieter veered off in his navy blue suit. He went down to the stream once more, to the place where shallow weirs had been made so people could wash their vegetables on the way home from the garden. Dieter wandered along. He didn't feel hungry and he needed to be alone. What would life be like without Oma? He walked beside the stream not watching where he was going. By the bridge he lost his footing and fell into the freezing mountain stream. He staggered out. Now he would have to go home. Although it was a warm spring day the snow melt in the stream set his teeth chattering.

When Dieter appeared, a forlorn, bedraggled child with his special suit clinging to him, he was soundly reprimanded by Mutti.

"Leave the child be! Here have some cake." He took the cake on a little round plate that Kathi offered him. He had looked forward to this delicious food for so long but now it had lost its appeal. He never dreamed that his celebration would turn out to be his Oma's wake.

The next morning Dieter had one thought in mind – to visit Oma's grave.

"You need something to eat. Here!" Mutti handed him his favourite food left over from the day before, two krapfen dusted with icing sugar. He took one in each hand and nibbled them as he wandered along. Oma's grave did not look so stark now that it had been filled in and covered with a blanket of flowers. But what was that at the end of the grave? Burrowed in amongst the flowers was Prinzl, their golden brown dachshund, head on his paws. Only his sad eyes turned towards Dieter to acknowledge his presence. Prinzl had been locked in Opa's shed at Zaugendorf, so how did he get here? Dieter sank to the ground beside him and put his arm round him, stroking his soft, silky ears.

"I know Prinzl, I know. I miss Oma so much too."

Later that day Rudi came to collect Prinzl and take him home. He coaxed and patted him but the little dog snapped when he tried to pick him up. Opa tried too but Prinzl would not budge. They left food and drink for him hoping he would come home when he was ready. Three days later Prinzl died at the foot of Oma's grave.

CHAPTER THIRTY-FOUR

Ding ding, ding ding! The angelus rang out cutting through Dieter's thoughts. He sat on a stool outside the door watching the play of light and shadow through the trees. The sun was beginning to set and a breeze riffled through the branches. He felt at peace when he could escape the cacophony inside the house. He dreamed of Oma and remembered the happy times.

"Pray for her soul and grow up to be a good man! That's all you can do for your Oma now." Father Schugmann had patted him on the head as he moved on to rap a girl over the knuckles for inattention. Dieter liked to picture Oma with the angels. Somehow it eased his pain.

The workers dwindled in from the fields after a day in the hot sun. Mr Zank drove his oxen in front of him with an occasional flick of the whip. The two oxen were yoked together and their heads were bowed as they pulled the wagon loaded with firewood. Dieter watched the wagon wheels roll over and over, crunching along the village street.

"Hallo," Mr Zank smiled as Dieter looked up.

After him came the town crier. He stopped down the road to read the news. "A meeting of the Council is to be held in the Council House on Wednesday evening at 7 pm sharp. Mr Schwarz has bought a new tractor. The pig market in Bamberg is coming up on the 30th May. If you want to buy or sell, be there!" He rattled it off without a pause and then rattled along to the next group of houses. I could do that, thought Dieter. Often he went to other houses in the village and gathered up to date news that never reached the Frankischer Daily. When the official crier had finished he would carry on. Surely people would be pleased to hear the rest of the news.

Dieter stood outside Mr Zank's large farm house with its overhanging roof. It was two storeys high and two refugee families shared rooms there. There was the potential for a sizeable audience here.

"St Florian's feast day on Wednesday. Remember to honour the patron saint of those who put out fires as well as the blacksmiths, chimney sweeps, brewers and potters. St Florian – Wednesday." To add emphasis he sang part of the church mass in his clear soprano voice. The entire Zank family stopped what they were doing and stood at open windows to listen. Mr Zank paused from unloading the wagon and doffed his cap at Dieter.

"Thank you Son."

He was a great success. From now on he would pass on important information too.

A few days later he was at it again.

"Did you hear Mrs Sueppl has died?"

"Really? How do you know?"

"The carpenter is making her coffin."

"God in heaven! I must do some baking." Mrs Schmidt made the sign of the cross as she closed her door. Dieter moved on.

"I'm sorry to tell you that Mrs Sueppl has died."

"No! When did this happen?"

"Last night."

"Are you sure?"

"Yes the carpenter is making her coffin."

So he continued stopping at homes where he felt they needed to know. He felt important bearing this momentous news. Mrs Sueppl had often been sick lately and he had seen the carpenter making her coffin. There was only one problem. The next morning Mrs Sueppl walked through the village to get some groceries and was met with a shocked silence.

"We heard you were dead," a brave woman finally stammered.

"Dead? Not for a year or two yet I hope. Who told you?"

So the tale was out! The next time Mrs Sueppl saw Dieter she warned him to make sure of his information before he spread false rumours. Well everything had pointed that way and it could have been true. How was he to know that the coffin was for someone in the next village. For a while Dieter stuck to songs he knew or reminders from the priest at Sunday Mass.

"The moon has risen
The stars are glimmering

The world is still and tired
And in some quiet chamber
A broken heart is weeping…..”

His voice soared to the high notes like a bird set free. No one questioned him then, only showed their appreciation. Well it could have been true.

CHAPTER THIRTY-FIVE

Time wandered along from house to house trying to keep up with Dieter. Mutti had moved to Gleusdorf and found new accommodation there but Dieter still returned to Muersbach and joined in activities with his old school mates. Today was Halloween and he had thought up a good idea in school. It was risky to think about such things in school and he had almost landed in hot water with the teacher. He just knew the older boys would think it was fantastic.

It was dusk as he joined the gang. Most of the birds were finished twittering and Dieter could smell the mangles as the boys scraped and hollowed them out. Helmut was looking after the candles.

"Hey I've got a good idea. Want to hear?"

"What is it?"

"We could put a mask on a stick and a sheet to cover the stick. That way we could reach the upstairs windows and give someone a really good fright."

"But how will you stop the mangle from sliding down?"

He hadn't thought of that. Trust Hermon to be difficult.

"Well ...." Dieter drew it out while his mind raced, "we could borrow a cross from the coffin maker." He was good friends with him and often stopped for a chat. Sometimes he was able to help the carpenter by lying in a coffin to see if it was the right size for a child. Now it reminded him of Oma when he did that and he felt sad again. So the carpenter owed him a favour he reasoned.

"All right, you go and ask."

Dieter shot off to see his friend. He had a bit of explaining to do. My word, the place smelled. Dieter wrinkled his nose and turned away from the stove where the horse hoof glue stewed. Finally the man relented but made Dieter promise to return the cross the next day. He showed it to his mates in triumph.

"See he didn't mind."

"Where are you going to use it?"

"I dunno," Dieter replied.

"Well I saw Friedl's parents going out. If you're quick you can scare Friedl before they get back."

"Right I'll go home and put it together." On the way Dieter borrowed a sheet from Kathi. Better not to ask Mutti for one, she might put the kibosh on it.

He leant the crucifix carefully against the house and hollowed out the mangle. Two triangles for eyes, an upside down triangle for a nose and ragged teeth in the mouth. He made a hole in the bottom for the crucifix and tied a candle to it. Next he draped the sheet over the cross arms and laughed to himself. This would scare the pants off Friedl. There was no time to lose. He hoped he wasn't too late.

"Nah, no problems!" his friends said."We'll come and watch."

They lit the candle and Dieter lifted it to the upstairs window where a light was burning. He tapped gently to get the occupant's attention. The lacy net curtain was pulled aside.

"Whoooo…." Dieter jiggled the apparition from side to side and up and down. Friedl shrieked as he drew back in alarm.

"Fantastic! Do it some more."

Dieter got bolder and louder with this encouragement and repeated the episode.

"Eeeeee…" his voice slid down the scale to make it more effective. It was! Friedl's screams rose to a crescendo.

Just then Mrs Trott opened her front door on the ground floor.

"Be off with you. Leave the poor boy alone. I'll tell your parents."

The group shot off round the corner and out of range. It had been most successful they agreed, until Mrs Trott stuck her nose in. Oh well they'd better call it a night.

Dieter decided to return the cross and the sheet on his way home. Then no questions would be asked. Better to get rid of the evidence just in case. However the next day Friedl's parents visited Mutti. There was no getting out of it.

"I'll make sure it won't happen again," she said as she shut the door. And she did.

CHAPTER THIRTY-SIX

"Today we are going to study how our ancestors lived."
Herr Nietschke had no trouble grabbing Dieter's attention. It was so interesting. Although Dieter missed his mates in Muersbach he enjoyed the way his new teacher taught class in Gleusdorf. The teacher had black hair slicked back with something that made his hair glisten in the sun. His fairisle jumper and corduroy trousers gave Herr Nietschke a more down to earth look than his previous teacher.

Dieter watched as he put up a canvas chart showing German tribes of 1000 years before. He used a long pointer to demonstrate how the tribes moved across Germany and where they settled. In awe he looked on as Herr Nietschke began to coil clay to represent them. He breathed in the damp mossy smell of the clay and wondered how long it had been part of the earth before his teacher dug it up.

"Their houses were low with a hole in the roof to let the smoke out." He placed a clay house on a board on his desk. "They made pots to cook their food on the fire. Like this." Coiling the clay as he spoke, he made an exquisite little cooking pot. How did he do it? He had Dieter's undivided attention. Now there was no time for daydreaming. Dieter was oblivious to the fidgeting and sniffing of the children around him. Time flew as Herr Nietschke took him back 1000 years and unfolded the ancient lifestyle with charts and models.

"There are books in the library about the Germanic tribes," he concluded.

Dieter couldn't wait to get a book and take it home to read. He would try and get in first when school had finished. That was another really good thing about Gleusdorf School – they had their very own library.

The History lesson had finished too soon.
"Now I'd like to hear some singing."

Dieter was well practiced at singing. As an impromptu town crier people often expressed appreciation of his clear soprano voice when he sang.

"Let's start with the little ones. They're usually the quietest."

Christa had started school now too. Usually Herr Nietschke sang a line of a song and then the class followed until they'd learnt the whole song. But today he felt like listening to the children one by one.

"How about the *Little Bird?* I like that one."

So one at a time the youngest children began to sing. The older children were standing at the back of the class. It was a bit of a hoot watching the little ones. Some were nervous and looked as though they might wet their pants. Others were confident and some couldn't even sing in tune. Well, it would pay not to be too critical because their turn would come soon enough. Christa was fourth in line. She looked up to the back of the class and saw her big brother there. She liked singing but she was a little nervous. Christa stood up straight and began to sing. It was a lovely tune and she soon overcame her fear and began to sing like the little bird. Dieter was surprised. He hadn't heard Christa sing on her own before. Singing was not something that happened in Mutti's house.

"Well done! Next!" Herr Nietschke smiled.

"She can't sing!" Dieter intended this for the ears of the boy next to him alone but Herr Nietschke's glance shot to the back of the room. A resounding voice boomed out.

"Sit down and be quiet."

Dieter had been put in his place. He was not the only one in the family who could sing.

CHAPTER THIRTY-SEVEN

It had not taken long to settle into life in Gleusdorf. As an outgoing, enterprising young fellow he soon found his way into the hearts and homes of the friendly villagers. When they moved to Gleusdorf Mutti had rented accommodation with the Nestmanns.

After school each day Christa was very conscientious with her homework. Dieter often watched her bent over her slate, tongue out the side of her mouth, practicing her writing. Dieter grudgingly admitted that she had a neat hand. But his writing was good enough and he had more important things to do. He needed to be out and about playing with the local children, keeping eyes and ears open to what was happening in the life of the village. Already he had developed a friendship with Sister Maria in the convent. Often she was out in the garden and would wrap her habit around him and smuggle him into the convent kitchen. She made him feel special and her closeness quieted his heart still beating loudly for Oma.

The kitchen was warm and inviting with soup bubbling on the stove and freshly baked bread cooling on a rack. It was torment when he first entered the room and his eyes and nose took in everything on offer. Dieter knew that he needed to say nothing. Sister Maria always came good.

"Here take this home for your family." Her eyes danced as she spoke. "Maybe bring a can tomorrow. We've got plenty of milk and I'm sure your mother could use extra with two little girls to feed and a growing lad like you." She patted his head. "Run along then and don't eat it all on the way home."

Sister Maria was a good standby but in autumn – that was something else! Dieter had long practice in sniffing out a pig killing. Everyone helped everyone else so it was easy to work out where the next occasion would be. When Dieter turned up the women had their sleeves rolled up and aprons over ample bosoms were tied around their waists. Firewood was stacked in the kitchen next to the copper which was beginning to steam. Their first job was to collect the pig's blood in large enamel bowls. Speed was needed to mix spices and finely chopped bacon fat into the blood before it congealed. Dieter watched as the women cleaned the intestines under running water and returned the bowls of blutwurst and sausage skins to the butcher to fill them. Everyone worked like clockwork. It was an age old tradition and the team moved from house to house as they were needed. With a twist of deft fingers the butcher made the sausage into a ring and placed it back in the bowl. Mrs Nestmann lowered them into the copper and stirred gently with a big wooden ladle. Dieter's stomach rumbled at the thought of the impending feast.

Other sausages were made the same way – fleischwurst, liverwurst, metwurst and presack. At the end of the day Dieter watched as the men carted wooden trays laden with sausages up the stairs to the attic. Here some were hung in the smoke house in a corner and others were hung elsewhere. But what was of most interest to Dieter was what remained in the kitchen. A copper full of kettle soup! After a whole day of boiling sausages in the copper it was rich and tasty. Dieter could count on getting a billy full of it, with maybe a ring or two of fleischwurst to take home to Mutti. It was really difficult to get a full can home and often he needed to drink some in case it spilled. Of course, once he started it was hard to stop. More than once Mutti sent him back.

"You'll have to go back for more. We'd like some too."

CHAPTER THIRTY-EIGHT

Between Muersbach and Gleusdorf there were fields of grain, mainly barley and wheat. From barley they made bread, beer and schnapps. The staples of life. Today harvesting was being done in Weber's fields, Dieter told Mutti.

"Let's go then and gather up what is left behind."

It was a lovely autumn day as Mutti, Dieter, Christa and her friend Trudl set off for the fields. Ingrid was perched on her big brother's shoulders where she had a good view of the scenery.

"Look Dieter, see the wagon." She patted his head to get his attention.

"Yes they're strong oxen, aren't they, and look at their horns."

Christa and Trudl skipped along behind. When they arrived the men had started swinging the scythes in determined arcs in front of them. They had completed one row and were moving back along the second with a practiced rhythm. It seemed effortless but Dieter knew that they had started early to avoid the hottest part of the day. Already he could see sweat glistening on their faces. Soon the women would begin their work, gathering the stalks of grain into sheaves and tying them up with some of the stalks. As they threw them aside young men came along and stacked the sheaves into stooks. Herr Weber whistled as he worked. It was a good crop this year and his family would be well provided for. He felt generous to the family who had come to pick up what the harvesters left behind.

"Leave a few extra ears of grain behind. They don't have much," he instructed the women. As they moved across the field he nodded to Erika and her children. "You can start now if you like."

"Thank you, Herr Weber."

Slowly Mutti and the children worked their way along the rows after the women had moved on. Ingrid played beside them in the stubble making little nests for the birds. It was back breaking work and Mutti stood up from time to time to stretch her back and look up at the sky. Werner, her husband, had gone again. She had not seen him for months and he had vowed he would not be back. With a sigh she bent to her task once again.

"This is how you do it. When you've got a good bundle tie it up like this." Dieter wrapped some stalks round and round his bundle and tucked the end in. He thought of the barley bread Mutti would make. He could smell it and taste it in anticipation. So they worked on till everyone in the field was called for morning tea.

"Brotzeit," called Herr Weber. A thick cloth was laid out in the wagon with slices of bread and butter on it. Fillings of sliced meats and cheeses sat nearby. Small barrels of beer and cider had been placed on the edge of the wagon so that the workers could help themselves. Herr Weber looked at the sky.

"Looks as though the weather will hold but I think we'll need to get it into the barn tonight."

The men nodded. Best to get it finished before they moved on to help someone else.

Then back to work. It was surprising how much Mutti and the children were gathering. They stacked their bundles at the end of each row away from the stooks.

Before they had finished the hay wagon trundled onto the field. The oxen patiently chewed their cuds, ruminating on the whole process. With the deft flick of a fork the men hiffed the stooks onto the wagon where they were stacked in an orderly fashion. Dieter helped his mother move their bundles out of the way.

"We don't want the oxen to stomp on them."

Mutti smiled. Dieter was a big help in looking after the family. More use to her than Werner!.

At the end of the day when the hay wagon had lurched homeward they each carried bundles of barley on their shoulders and headed off. Dieter held Ingrid's hand.

"You'll have to walk home now but Mutti will make us some lovely barley bread tomorrow. Think about that."

Once home Mutti prepared a quick meal for her and the children. Trudl headed off and Ingrid went happily to bed. It was near the end of the summer holidays so there was no school tomorrow. Dieter and Christa were keen to help Mutti finish the task. Mutti spread a sheet out in the middle of the floor and Christa straightened the corners.

Each of them stood over the sheet and rubbed ears of barley between their hands, back and forth to get the grain out. They put the stalks that were left to one side. It was a tedious job but they did not have access to the village threshing machine like the farmers. The little pile of barley began to grow while the stack of bundles began to dwindle. At last they were finished.

"A cup of cocoa and then into bed." Mutti beamed at them as she set a saucepan of milk on the stove. "You've done a grand job."

"Can I help you take the barley to the mill tomorrow?"

"Of course you can."

Dieter wanted to make sure there were no unnecessary delays in turning the grain into tasty bread. The miller would weigh the grain and exchange it for the same weight in barley flour.

"We'll have fresh barley bread tomorrow."

"Mmmm," was the only reply as two pairs of eyes looked at her over their cups of cocoa.

CHAPTER THIRTY-NINE

Summer was turning to autumn with the leaves beginning to change colour. Soon there would be heaps of dry leaves for them to scrunch through on their way home from school, Dieter thought. He wondered what Mutti would have for them to eat when he got home today. Opening the door he walked in and put his bag on the hook behind the door.

"Hello Mutti." No answer, just a sniff. She was washing dishes in the sink with her back to Dieter. She was banging the plates around as she put them on the rack. Beside her on the bench was a chopping board with a partly chopped onion sitting in its juice. Was the onion at fault or was she upset? He would need to tread carefully here. No taking off to play.

"What's to eat?" He tried to sound cheerful, not demanding.

"Get what you want. There's bread there." Mutti turned her puffy face towards him. This was more than onions. "What's wrong Mutti?" She pulled an envelope from her apron pocket.

"This is what's wrong. Werner's dead. Motorbike accident. Gone. No more." She started to sob. Dieter looked at the letter as she waved it in front of him distractedly. Her name was typed on the envelope, that much he could see. So it was an official letter.

"Who told you?"

"This is from the Court. Now I get no more money to look after me and the girls. How will we survive?"

"We'll think of something," Dieter said in a calming tone.

"It says to go to Ebern to the office there but they'll want to know all my business. It's not fair."

"Let's talk to Opa. He'll know what to do."

"He's got enough on his mind." She sat at the table beside Dieter staring at the letter and sniffing from time to time.

"First he divorces me, now this. Never did take his responsibility seriously."

It sounded as though she blamed Werner for having an accident. He had not been living there since Dieter came home to live, not that he cared. He did not have any pleasant memories of Werner. Dieter swallowed a mouthful of bread with a gulp. It stuck in his gullet. How could he help? Oh, he wished Oma was still alive.

"You run along and play. I'll think of something. And bring Christa home at dinner time. She's playing at Trudl's."

Dieter went out with a heavy heart. What would happen to them now? He went down to the stream alone and threw stones in the water. He needed to think. Slowly he walked along the bank watching the water trickle between the stones and flow over the moss covered rocks. He threw a stick in and watched it twist and turn as the water took it where it would. His life was like that. He did not have any say in what happened and he certainly felt helpless as he was tossed this way and that. Finally he heard the angelus ring out and knew he should find Christa and go home. Christa chattered on, not noticing that her big brother was very quiet. He opened the door and let her go inside first.

"I've had an idea," Mutti said brightly. "I don't want charity from busy bodies. I'm going to advertise. There must be a kind man out there who wants some security. We could start again."

Well! Dieter was speechless. It was not his decision anyway but he hoped it would work. He was relieved that Mutti's mood had changed. At least she had stopped crying.

That evening when the children were in bed Mutti struggled with her composition. Finally she was satisfied.

WANTED

Kind, loving man with a view to marriage

Please reply in writing to

Untermerzbacher Street Number 6, Gleusdorf

As she licked the envelope and sealed it with a thump of her fist she smiled. She was quite capable of making her way in life. Pulling a scarf over her head she hustled out the door and down to the post box. The children would be all right. She would not be long.

The letter was on its way. Dear God, she prayed, may the right man see my advertisement. Each day Mutti watched as the postman went by. She watched to see if he sailed past or slowed down to post an answer through the slot in her door. But no, day after day there was no reply. Maybe she was expecting an answer too soon. It may have taken a while for the newspaper cogs to turn. She would not give up yet.

One afternoon several weeks later there was a knock on her door. Who could it be? She took off her apron, wiped her hands on it and stuffed it in a cupboard out of sight. Smoothing her hair she walked to the door.

"Hallo. I'm Guenter." A young man stood there looking very nervous and shy.

"Yes?"

"I've come in reply to your advertisement in the newspaper."

"Well you'd better come in then. I'm Erika."

She ushered him into the kitchen. He looked at Ingrid playing with blocks on the floor.

"That's Ingrid. She's two."

Hallo Ingrid." She glanced at him and went on with her play.

Erika could not think where to start. It was much easier when she met someone somewhere and then just started up a conversation. This was different. She had not given it much thought. Should she interview him or what? He looked all right so that was a start. She decided not to tell him about her other two children until it was time for them to come home from school. Maybe by then he would have thawed out a bit.

"So Guenter, would you like a coffee?"

"Yes please. That sounds good."

Erika bustled around making the coffee and put a plate of cake in front of him.

"Thank you."

Gradually they talked. Guenter was twenty-three years old and was not married. He came from a farm near Koblenz and was keen to move away from home and start a new life. He was shy, could not find a girl he said and then he saw Erika's advertisement. Erika told him a little about herself. She mentioned that Werner had gone off with another woman and left her in the lurch with three children. She did not confess to the fact that only Ingrid was Werner's child. There had been Max, then Emil (both his children had not survived, Monika died at 6 weeks and the little boy was stillborn.) After that came Christa's father Franz, then Werner. He had divorced her and had recently been killed in a motorbike accident, she told him.

"Three children?" Guenter sounded rather hesitant at this.

"Oh, they're good children, past the baby stage now. They're no trouble. Dieter and Christa will be home from school soon."

"How old are they?"

"Dieter's ten and Christa is six."

He looked thoughtful as he sipped his coffee.

Soon Christa and Dieter came in from school.

"Ooh, cake. Can I have some please?"

"Yes when you've put your bag away and left your dirty shoes outside."

Dieter looked at his shoes. He had mud on them from traipsing along by the stream.

"This is Guenter."

"Hallo." Two pairs of eyes looked solemnly at him.

"You'll have dinner with us won't you?"

Erika wished she'd had more warning but it could not be helped. Seeing he hadn't written first he would have to take things as they were. It wasn't her fault. He seemed nice enough and she wanted to get to know him better. She wondered if anyone else would respond to her advertisement.

At dinner that night Dieter and Christa were unusually quiet. They had never seen this man before. After everything was cleaned up they were packed off to bed.

"Dieter will read you a story."

They piled into their bed and Dieter took out his library book from school.

"This is a story about Siegfried who lived a long time ago."

As he read on it was not long before Ingrid was asleep and soon after Christa too. Good, he could read to himself for a while. From the other room he could hear the muted voices of Mutti and Guenter talking. Dieter felt as though Guenter was an intruder. Opa and Oma had never invited strangers in like this. Finally the book slipped from his hands onto the floor and Dieter too had succumbed to sleep.

In the morning Dieter woke to hear Guenter pleading with Mutti to let him stay.

"Please, please Erika. I'll get a job and look after you and the children."

She had hoped to have a selection, more than one to choose from. But what if Guenter was the only one who replied? Finally Erika relented.

What was she thinking? Dieter did not like Guenter. He was a stranger and Mutti had let him stay all night. To make matters worse the children were told to call him Papa Guenter.

"Papa Guenter? Even in front of my school friends?"

"Yes you will show him respect."

So Dieter, Christa and Ingrid had gained a stepfather.

Opa had nothing to say. He had given up long ago. She seemed to go from one man to another, discarded them like clothes she had grown out of. Her father just wished that Erika would do the right thing by the children, one day. In the meantime he would keep an eye on her man from a distance.

Eventually Erika and Guenter were married by Father Wunderle at his insistence.

"You need to make a decent woman of her," he said.

CHAPTER FORTY

As he settled onto the slatted wooden seat on the train next to the window, Dieter was glad of his thick snow pants that gave him some padding. The small framed window was covered in snowflake patterned ice which was fascinating. Dieter took off a mitten and traced it with his finger, his face close to the grimy window. His breath fogged the window allowing in a diffused light for more patterns to be made. It reminded him of Oma and the 'little people' she used to tell him about. When he was younger he would look for their doorways to homes under the roots of trees in the forest. He had spent many happy hours looking for their haunts and noticing how they decorated their doorways. They paint ice patterns on our windows, she used to say. He wondered how they survived out in such wintry weather but presumed their long hair and beards helped to keep them warm, as well as hats pulled down over their ears, long coats, fur-lined boots and mittens. It was a pleasant memory. Now there was a round patch in the window where the icicles had melted and he could see the landscape rocketing past.

"Here's some bread and sausage." Mutti's voice broke into his reverie. She handed him some dark bread and broke off a piece of wurst.

"I'm not very hungry just now."

"Well it'll be the last you get for a while."

Reluctantly he took it and nibbled the end as he turned his gaze back to the window and beyond. He had been in hospital with pneumonia for over a week and his appetite had not returned yet. He did not know where they were going and he had not bothered to ask. They were on their way to 'a better life' was all his mother had said.

"Don't make a mess. Keep your jacket clean," his mother continued.

"Yes Mutti." What was all the fuss about? The little girls were more likely to make a mess than an eleven year old. Christa moved closer to her big brother and snuggled up to keep warm.

"Mind my jacket! Mutti, she's dirtying my jacket."

"All right. All right. Just move over a bit Christa. Would you like some milk?" She took a flask from her knapsack and passed it to Dieter. "Leave enough for your sisters."

"Yes Mutti." He took a mouthful, wiped his mouth with the back of his hand and handed it to Ingrid.

"What about me? It's my turn," grumbled Christa.

"Just wait will you," Guenter put in.

Calm returned to the carriage and Dieter put his arm around Christa. Most of the time it was good being with his sisters but it had taken some getting used to them.

His memory of last night was hazy as he'd fallen into bed exhausted. They had left Hanau early in the morning. He was pleased to move on because Hanau reminded him of the camps that he had slept in with Oma and Opa before they settled in Zaugendorf. It had taken all day, a long endless day, clickety-clacketing north through the flat winter landscape. Everything had been covered in snow and trees tried in vain to reach upward and warm their limbs in the thin sunshine that shone now and then. Dieter had felt the biting cold through the train window. Inside the carriage was not much warmer but they were well wrapped up in thick snow jackets and trousers. Dieter's pilot helmet was buttoned under his chin and he wriggled his fingers inside his mittens to keep them warm. Night had closed in around them and still they had rattled on, lulled into a sense of peace. At last the train pulled into a siding with a hiss and a sigh.

Mutti fussed around the children buttoning jackets and checking that they still had their cards strung around their necks. 'MV Fairsea' it said, '20 February 1954.' Underneath was a large K with a blank below. Dieter's job was to hold a sister on each hand and make sure they did not get lost, while Guenter carried their meager belongings in a battered brown suitcase. Mutti was in charge of proceedings. They had followed her along a boardwalk into a large brightly lit doorway. Dieter did not care where he went as long as he could stretch out on a bed soon and go to sleep.

"Go to the table marked K," she said as the four of them had stopped at 'G'.

Dieter mutely obeyed and presented his card to the officer. 'Bed 8' he wrote and 'Table 2'. With a nod to a waiting man he said, "Follow him." Dieter stumbled along into a narrow passage. His boots clanged on the sharp metal stairs as they descended below. It must be a large camp, he thought. All of the camps they had been in since leaving Sudetenland were single storeyed but that was a long time ago. They wound down three flights and at last he was shown his bunk with two army blankets folded on the end. Two more bunks rose to the ceiling above him. When Dieter turned the man had gone. He did not bother to take off his boots or jacket, just his hat. Wrapping a blanket around himself he flopped onto the bed, too tired to care where the rest of his family might be. He would find them in the morning. Dieter drifted into an easy sleep in spite of the hubbub and naked lights overhead.

As morning crept in Dieter woke with a start. He sat up and bumped his head on the bunk above. Where was he? He scratched his tousled hair and rubbed his eyes. A dull thudding came from below. Another more insistent noise disturbed his ears. Where was it coming from? All around him in the large room men and boys slept, snored, grunted and stirred. Minding his head Dieter stood on the floor, straightened his rumpled clothes, put on his hat and moved quietly out into the passage. At the end he saw a metal stairway leading upward on a sharp angle. Dieter followed, clinging to the rail as he climbed. He was puffed after winding up three flights of stairs and stumbled out into the bright daylight. It shocked him as he realized he was on the deck of a ship. Moving to the rail he scanned the horizon. Ahead he saw the dark outline of an icebreaker clearing a path for them into the North Sea. The air was freezing and his breath hung in a cloud in front of him. The clank and screech of metal he had heard below was an icebreaker ploughing its way through solid ice. Reflected light from the ice and snow caused him to squint into the distance.

Slowly the sounds on the deck around him trickled into his consciousness. A woman with a scarf tied under her chin wailed loudly as she looked back to Bremen receding behind them. Her husband tried vainly to console her, patting her shoulder with his stubby hand. Dieter felt like crying but there was no one to comfort him. A group of men discussed where they might be going.

"I reckon we're headed for Canada," said the fat one.

"No Franz, more likely South America."

"We'll know we are bound for Australia if we see the Southern Cross."

"No chance of that for a while!" put in Franz.

"Ja, need to cross the Equator first."

Dieter's heart sank. He had no idea where he was, let alone where he was going. What about Opa? When would he see him again? Would he ever see Rudi again? Oma's grave was fresh in his mind. He had promised himself he would plant lily of the valley on it this spring. His thoughts weighed him down like a thick, wet overcoat. The smell of diesel wafted from the funnel. A long mournful tone from the icebreaker startled him from his troubled reverie. The Fairsea replied with its ship's horn as the icebreaker turned and headed back to its haven. Dieter clasped his jacket to his chest and descended the stairs to his bunk room.

Where else was there to go!

ABOUT THE AUTHOR

Jean Klier was born in New Zealand where she lived for the first twenty years of her life. After training as a primary teacher she left New Zealand to teach in the Western Highlands of Papua New Guinea where she met and married Dieter. Travels to other places followed and they are now retired and living in Albury, New South Wales, Australia with an adorable but nutty dog Peanut. Their three adult children and four grand children are scattered around Australia and New Zealand.

Torn Apart is Jean's first novel and is the first one of a series of four books.

If you enjoyed reading **Torn Apart** you may want to find out what happened next. See over for a preview of the second book in the series –**The Alien Nation**.

THE ALIEN NATION

CHAPTER ONE

It was very cold on deck but Dieter found comfort in the freedom there. He had become used to the routine on board over the last couple of days and knew his way round especially to the dining room.
"Where are we now?" he asked one of the crew members.
"Heading for the Bay of Biscay. That's where some people get real sick."
"Well I'm all right," Dieter grinned.
"Yeah, but we're not there yet."
Dieter walked over to the port side and leant on the rails. He loved to watch the sea churning as the ship slid through the water, powered by chugging engines. He noticed when the ship began to nod and roll a little. Yes, there was a change in the motion but he felt just fine.
"Breakfast is now served in the dining room," a voice boomed over the loud speaker. Good! He needed food to start the day. Down the metal stairs he went. He sat at a table and waited to be served.
"What is it today?"
"Bacon and eggs with toast. Want some?"
"Yes please."
Dieter breathed in appreciatively as the food was placed in front of him. It smelled delicious. He looked around for Papa Guenter but he was not there. Maybe he would come later. It didn't matter. Someone else would talk to him. First he settled down to the job at hand and tucked in to his breakfast. Mmmmm it was good.

It seemed pretty stuffy in the dining room today but maybe it was merely the difference between the fresh air on deck and being downstairs. Maybe they had turned the heating up. Dieter had almost finished his breakfast when the ship began to roll more. Now he knew why they had an edging around the table. He slowed down with his egg and toast, was no longer sure that he could finish it. No, he decided, he had better leave the rest. Hanging onto the table he got to his feet and took his plate back to the servery. He felt quite unsteady as he walked past tables.
"Not so good?" the cook asked.

"No."

"You'd best go and lie down then."

"Yes."

Dieter made his way down below. His stomach seemed to turn somersaults as the ship plowed on. Dieter made a detour to the toilets and relieved himself of his breakfast.

"Oh, dear God." He thought of Oma as he fell onto the bed. He felt dreadful. Sometime later Guenter appeared.

"You sick?"

"Mm, I feel bad."

"Don't worry. It won't last long."

Well it did. It lasted for eight days. Sometimes he slept. Other times Guenter and the steward propped him up and encouraged him to sip water which had something in it. Was it salt? Or sugar? Other times it was clear soup. He wished they would leave him alone, just let him die. But no, they persisted. His days were punctuated with the clang of shoes on the metal stairs. He felt trapped in the belly of the ship like a baby in the womb. No choice, no escape. A naked light shone in the daytime, lightening up the grey steel walls. He could hear the water roiling past and the staccato announcements over the loud speakers at meal times. Each time his stomach churned at the thought of food.

Finally it began to abate. One afternoon he waited and listened for the steward to bring him some soup.

"Sitting up waiting are we? That's a good sign."

"Yes I'm hungry." He drank it in small sips as he had been told. He didn't want any repeats.

"Can I have some more?"

"We'll wait a bit and see how you go. Not good to have too much in a hurry." The steward sat on his bunk and talked to him.

"Where are we going? What country?"

"Off to Australia. It's much warmer there."

"Australia." It helped a little to know where you were going but at the same time Dieter could not help looking back.

"They have funny animals in Australia." The steward felt the need to lighten the conversation. "Kangaroos that hop along on great big back legs with strong tails sticking out behind them. Like this." He hopped the length of the bunk and back again. Dieter laughed.

"Is that true?"

"Yes. God's honour. I'll die if I tell a lie! And koalas too."

"What's a koala?"

"It's a grey furry animal that climbs trees. Well it lives in a gum tree and eats nothing but gum leaves. It sleeps in the tree too."

"How do you know all this?"

"I watched a film on Australia once."

"I'll see those animals when I get there, I suppose."

Yes you will, but how about a little more soup and that will do for today. Tomorrow I think you can go back on deck and then to the dining room for meals."

"That'll be good."

The next day Dieter was able to go on deck and then to the dining room. He felt a bit wobbly on it but with solid food and sea air he soon got his sea legs. He gained his independence again and made friends. That lad always seems to be on his own, not with his family, others sometimes remarked about him..

"Well when I'm older I'll get a job in Australia so I can save up and go back to Germany where most of my family lives," was all he would say when asked.

CHAPTER TWO

It was just before sundown. Life was much better back on deck. The ship was passing through the Straits of Mesina in the Mediterranean Sea. To starboard Dieter looked at the lights high on the hills, dotted among the vineyards and olive groves. On the port side fewer lights were visible on the lower reaches of the coastline. It was amazing that he could see two landscapes from his vantage point as they moved through the Straits. He breathed in the smell of wood-smoke as fires burned the prunings from the terraced vineyards. In a flash the pure smell of wood burning took him back to memories of Oma at the stove cooking his food. They were warm comforting memories but he had no one to share them with.

The golden sun reflected off the cliffs leaving reddish brown scars in the shade. It was cooler now but the men were playing music on the deck enjoying the lingering light – accordions and harmonicas mostly.

"What next?" one of the men asked.

"Play what you like," an onlooker replied.

After a discussion together they began to play:

Today on board
Tomorrow away
Homeland adieu
High the waves roll
Homeward gulls fly
Ship on high seas.

Everyone joined in and it sounded very jolly. Dieter however was glad when they changed to sea songs from Northern Germany and popular songs of the day. At least they were not so melancholy. With his mother suffering from sea sickness and expecting a baby, Guenter spent all his time looking after Mutti and Dieter's two sisters. There was no one to share how he was feeling. He found a vacant deck chair and settled back, listening to the murmur of voices and the rollicking songs. The Fairsea plowed on, inexorably widening the gap between Germany and everyone on board. He may as well be travelling alone. Dieter tried to imagine what life would be like in Australia until sleep lured him into its arms. He dreamed of home in

Zaugendorf in their packing case cottage built by Opa. They were sitting around the stove in the evening and Oma was singing to Opa and Dieter, a song of Opa's homeland. He could hear her soft lilting voice as she sang the Sudeten Mountain Song.

Blue mountains, green valleys
Nestled there a little house
Loveliest place on earth
And there is my home
When once I roamed this land
The mountains gazed on me
Through my childhood, through my youth
I know not how this happened to me.

O my lovely Sudeten Mountains
Where the Elbe quietly flows
Where Rubezahl and his little people
Still their legends and fairytales spin
Sudeten Mountains, Gothic mountains
You are my beloved homeland.

Opa reached out and stroked her face as she smiled at him.
"Everybody up! Move back!"
Where was he? Dieter woke up with a start. That's right, he was on the ship going to Australia……..

TORN APART

JEAN KLIER